Listen for the Singing

Also by Jean Little

From Anna
Hey World, Here I Am!
Kate
Look Through My Window
Stand in the Wind

Listen for the Singing

JEAN LITTLE

HarperTrophy
A Division of HarperCollinsPublishers

The publisher and author gratefully acknowledge permission to quote from the following verses:

"In Flanders Field" on pages 154 and 155. Reproduced by permission of *Punch*.

"I never saw a moor" on page 60. "I'm nobody. Who are you?" on pages 123–124, and "He ate and drank the precious words" on page 257 by Emily Dickinson. Reprinted from *Poems* by Emily Dickinson, edited by Martha Dickinson Bianchi and Alfred Leete Hampson, Little, Brown and Company.

"Over the Rainbow" on pages 142 and 143, by Harold Arlen and E. Y. Harburg. Copyright 1938, 1939, renewed 1966, 1967 Metro-Goldwyn-Mayer. Rights throughout the world controlled by Leo Feist, Inc. Used by permission.

Listen for the Singing
Copyright © 1977, 1991 by Jean Little

Typography by Joyce Hopkins
New Edition

Library of Congress Cataloging-in-Publication Data
Little, Jean, date
  Listen for the singing / Jean Little.—New ed.
    p.   cm.
  Summary: As the world around her braces itself for World War II, a young Canadian girl with impaired vision prepares to begin public high school.
  ISBN 0-06-023910-7 (lib. bdg.)   0-06-440394-7 (pbk.)
  [1. Physically handicapped—Fiction.   1. Brothers and sisters—Fiction. 3. High schools—Fiction.   4. Schools—Fiction.]   I. Title.
PZ7.L7225Li   1991b   90-40019
[Fic]—dc20   CIP
                                                                        AC

Published in hardcover by HarperCollins Publishers.
First Harper Trophy edition, 1991.

for Ellen S. Rudin, my editor
and
for Ellen, my friend

So many people helped me with various aspects of the research necessary for this book. I wish I could thank each one of you individually, but there are just too many. You know who you are. Thank you all.

My special thanks go to Tamara Puthon, who is in charge of research at the Guelph Public Library. She answered countless questions from her desk and also read the manuscript through carefully at home, checking it for errors. It was she who told me what Germans might eat for breakfast, the exact time war was declared, where Hitler was born, whether there are skylarks in Germany, what meats taste best with sauerkraut, and a hundred other things. Thank you, Tamara, for your ready help and your unflagging interest.

—Jean Little

Listen for the Singing

1

ANNA WAKENED TO HEAR someone walking from the bathroom back along the hall.

"Is that you, Papa?" she said.

She did not need to ask. Even half asleep, she knew his step.

"Yes. Go back to sleep, child. I'm sorry I disturbed you."

"I was awake already." It wasn't a lie exactly, just a polite fib. "Why are you up so early?"

This time, he made no reply. Anna, from the curtained-off alcove that served as her bedroom, heard him going back down the stairs.

3

She was settling down, preparing to doze off again, when she realized that this might be the very chance she had been hoping for: time alone with her father. As far back as she could remember, whenever she was in trouble too big to handle alone, she had gone to him for help. The two of them were so close that often he understood before she was well into her explanation. And if ever she were facing trouble, it was right now, looking ahead to school beginning on Tuesday morning. Maybe Papa could think of some way to make it less terrifying or her more courageous. Even if he couldn't, simply talking it over with him would help. She could count on him to take her seriously when someone else might scoff.

But could she? Hadn't Papa changed lately? When had he last taken time to listen to her as though she mattered to him in a special way?

"Papa's Pet," her big brother Rudi used to call her. He had teased and taunted her with other names too—Awkward Anna, Dummkopf, Pickle Face, Little Stupid, and always Baby because she was the youngest. Those mean names had hurt and humiliated her, making her sometimes feel as awkward and stupid as Rudi said she was. "Papa's Pet," however, she had never minded. Each time he said it she smiled inside, knowing it was true.

At least, it had been true. Now . . . ?

It's still true, she told herself sharply. It's only that Papa's been so worried about the news. I'd better get down there before the paperboy comes!

Before she sat up even, she reached for her glasses and put them on. The world around her, a blurred, unreal place before, sprang into sharper focus as she looked at it through the thick lenses. Suddenly she was able to distinguish the pinkish stripes in the faded wallpaper, the many-colored squares in her patchwork quilt, the kitchen chair on which she had laid her library book facedown, open at her place. Less clearly, she could make out the chest of drawers at the foot of her bed and the tall, narrow wardrobe jammed up against it, in which her dresses hung.

Although she had worn glasses for nearly five years, it still astonished her that she had ever managed without them. Now, putting them on was the way she started every day, and she did not take them off, except to clean them, until she was in bed for the night. Even while she slept she kept them placed within easy reach.

But this was no time to be thinking about her eyes!

She got out of bed and was feeling about for her slippers when she heard something that made her stop and listen.

Please, let it be only my imagination, she prayed. Please, don't let it . . .

Her prayer went unanswered. She heard it again, an unmistakable, all-too-familiar, sharp crackle of sound. Static! Papa had turned on his detestable radio! She was already too late to talk to him.

Anna climbed back into bed. She punched her pillow

to make it the right shape to lean back against. Then she pulled the sheet over her knees and sat glaring into space. No, she was glaring at her father, even though he could not see her. She could see him! She did not have to be in the same room to know exactly what he was doing and how he looked doing it. She must have seen him a million times. He was sitting in the shabby, sagging arm-chair, his head bent close to the big shortwave set he had bought for himself over a year ago, his face closed off from everyone and everything around him as he listened to the latest news broadcast.

How amazed they had all been the night he brought that radio home, Papa who never bought anything for himself unless Mama made him. The set was expensive too, even though he had got it secondhand.

"Is the Depression over?" Fritz blurted out, staring at it.

Everyone understood why he asked. For years and years, there had been hard times. There was always enough to eat, but seldom second helpings. There had been no money for extras for anyone. How Anna had begged for an Eaton Beauty doll the Christmas she was ten! Till Mama told her sharply to stop hurting Papa by asking him for something he couldn't afford to get for her. Yet, that night, there stood Papa with this big shiny radio!

"No, the Depression's not over. Not yet," her father had said, clearing a place of honor for his new possession. "But it will be before long."

6

"When?" Fritz asked.

"When the war begins," Papa answered matter-of-factly.

As though he knew there was no way out, Anna thought now, with the same quick shiver of fear she had felt that evening. Yet so far there was still a depression and Canada was not at war.

Of course, there was some fighting going on in Europe. Over the last many months, Anna had seen it in newsreels at the movies. They showed Adolf Hitler screaming speeches at wildly cheering mobs, German troops goose-stepping and giving the now famous "Heil, Hitler!" salute, and German forces moving across borders to occupy neighboring countries.

As she sat in the darkened theater and watched the flickering black-and-white pictures, Anna felt nothing in common with the people she saw there, even though she and her family had come from Germany to Canada only five years ago. She dimly remembered a time when Frankfurt had seemed the whole world and German the language everyone spoke. Now Toronto was the real place, and she spoke, thought, and even dreamed in English. The hysteria of the German people caught by the newsreel camera mystified her as much as it did the rest of the audience. Papa claimed it was a madness that threatened the peace of the world, but Mama scoffed at such foreboding. Anna did not know what to think. If Mama went to the movies and saw for herself, she might be more

7

afraid. Still, it was all happening on the far side of an immense ocean.

The day before yesterday, German soldiers had invaded Poland. All that meant to Anna, right at this minute, was that Papa was too worried to remember that she, his youngest, his "pet," was about to start high school—and she was terrified at the prospect.

How can he forget? she thought, feeling betrayed by her father for the first time in her life. I'll bet he doesn't know a single, solitary person in Poland!

Downstairs the clock chimed the hour. Anna counted the strokes. Why, it was only six o'clock! Papa must be crazy.

She yawned. It was far too early to be awake. She slid down a little so her head rested against the pillow. She would go back to sleep after all, since Papa had no time to spare.

What was that? Had someone cried out?

"Klara! Klara, come!"

Then, before that made any sense to her, Anna heard her father calling from the foot of the stairs.

"Rudi! Anna, wake Rudi. Call everyone. Quickly! Do you hear me, Anna?"

"Yes, Papa."

Springing out of bed, Anna ran not to waken the others but to stand where she could look down from the landing. Her father had not waited. He was back in the living room. She could hear, faintly, a slow measured voice speaking. Not Papa's. A British voice. Frightened, she strained to catch the words:

". . . God bless you all and may He defend the right."

"Papa," she cried out, starting down to him, "what is it? What's wrong?"

Her father appeared in the doorway that joined the living room to the front hall. Anna, two steps down, stopped where she was and stared at him. What had happened? He stooped as though he were old, old or sick. He looked like a stranger.

"It's come. Britain has declared war on Germany," Ernst Solden said.

So Papa had been right. All those times, when he had warned them war must come, and Mama had been angry with him for talking so foolishly—he had been right. For one instant, Anna felt glad, glad her mother had been the foolish one and her father the one who really knew. Stunned by what he had just told her, still not really understanding anything of what it meant, she almost smiled.

Then the light from the window shone full on her father's face and, in spite of her poor vision, she saw the shine of tears on his cheeks.

She fled back up the stairs.

2

"RUDI!" SHE SHOUTED, flinging open the door to the boys' bedroom. "Rudi, wake up. Wake up!"

Fritz reared up wide awake, but Rudi did not even open his eyes.

"Why?" he asked, his voice thick with sleep and profoundly uninterested.

Anna's fear vanished; excitement rose up in its place. For once in her life, she had the advantage over her oldest brother.

"There's a WAR!" she announced. She felt like someone in a play, a messenger with one crucial line to say. "Papa says to come downstairs. Hurry!"

She dashed along the hall to rouse her sisters. How shocked, how disbelieving their two faces were as she hurled her news at them! How wonderful that she had been the first to know.

"Hurry up," she urged, glorying in being bossy while simply obeying Papa.

She rushed down the stairs. Rudi was already there, standing next to Papa, both of them listening to the radio.

"Where's Mama?" she asked.

"I called her. Isn't she here?" Papa said. He did not even look around to see.

Her parents' bedroom was downstairs, on the other side of the dining room. Anna opened the door and saw her mother deep in sleep. She went up to the bed and put her hand on Mama's shoulder, the way she used to when she was little and felt sick in the night. For anything else she went to Papa, but Mama was best when you were sick. Klara Solden came awake at once, as Anna knew she would.

"What's wrong?" she asked, raising herself on her elbow and peering at her youngest with worried eyes.

"Papa wants you," Anna said. "He got up early to listen to the news because of Poland. . . ."

"That man!" Mama snorted. "As if we don't have enough troubles of our own."

"Mama," Anna said, steeling herself, "it's war now. Britain against Germany. Just like Papa said."

She had braced herself for nothing. Mama got up qui-

11

etly, put on her robe, and automatically ran a comb through her hair.

Anna stood by, wondering what she should be doing.

"Come," Mama said, stretching out her hand to take Anna's. They went together to the living room. Fritz and Frieda were there too, and Gretchen was hurrying down the stairs.

"What Anna has said . . . she has it wrong somehow?" Klara Solden asked her husband.

"Listen," Papa said. "They're rebroadcasting Mr. Chamberlain's speech."

Anna knew Mr. Chamberlain was the Prime Minister of Britain. He was the one who had gone to meet with Hitler at the conference in Munich and come back promising England "peace in our time." Papa had called him a blind fool because he had believed Hitler would keep the promises he made not to invade any more of Europe.

Fool or not, he sounded tired and sad to Anna. She recognized his as the voice she had heard earlier:

"May God bless you all and may He defend the right."

Before the speech was over, Mama had collapsed into Papa's chair in tears. Papa put his arm awkwardly around her shoulders. The announcer's voice went on, but finally Papa had ceased to listen.

"Can I turn it off, Papa?" Rudi asked, looking at his mother. "There won't be anything new for a while, I guess."

Papa nodded. Anna watched Rudi take a step forward.

12

His hand fumbled and it was a second before he could silence the announcer's voice. He jerked his hand away and knotted it together with his other one behind his back. Anna, startled, stared at him, but although he looked stern and perhaps pale, how else would he look? War! She tried to make it have some reality for herself. It still seemed something Papa talked about, something far away, nothing to do with her.

Like Judgment Day, Anna thought, and was glad the others couldn't see into her mind.

"Will we still have to start school on Tuesday?" asked Fritz.

A wild hope sprang up in Anna. But Rudi reacted unexpectedly again by snapping at his brother, before Papa had a chance to answer.

"Of course we will. Don't be such a fool!"

Anna took off her glasses, polished them hurriedly on a fold of her nightgown, and put them back on. Through them, she stared at Rudi again. Was he really as angry as he sounded? He did look fierce, ready to fight with somebody.

"What use would you be in a war? You or any other kid?" Rudi raged on as though Fritz was arguing.

Before Fritz could come to his own defense, Papa answered the fear behind Rudi's words.

"You are barely eighteen, Rudi. Of course you will continue your education."

Mama gasped, her horrified glance leaping from man

13

to boy. Anna felt confused until she heard Rudi say loudly, his voice scornful, "I was not thinking of myself."

She knew he was lying. He had never been able to lie successfully. And she wanted to laugh at the silliness of her brother imagining that anybody would want him to leave school to fight.

Fritz would be a far better choice. Rudi couldn't even peel a potato without cutting his finger. He was good-looking. He could work out complicated abstract problems in his head. Gretchen assured them he was a terrific dancer. He talked well.

But he wasn't a soldier. As far as Anna could see, Mama had nothing to worry about.

"They might start school a day late or something," Fritz muttered. "That's all I meant."

Nobody paid any attention to him this time.

Rudi had started to whistle through his teeth, not loudly, but tonelessly so that it grated on your ears. He had raised his head now and was gazing fixedly at something outside the front window. Anna looked too but saw only a blur of white curtains and the early-morning light. Of course, Rudi could see much better than she could, even with her glasses, but she had a feeling he was not looking at anything just as he was not whistling anything.

"I'll fix some breakfast," Gretchen said suddenly, taking up the burden of being the eldest daughter. "Aren't you hungry, Mama?"

14

Mama did not seem to have heard her. She was looking at the silent radio.

"Ernst," she said, "could there have been a mistake?"

"You heard it yourself, Klara," her husband answered simply.

"I can't understand it," she said.

Frieda turned her head away from her mother's dazed face. "I'll help you, Gretchen."

The two girls moved slowly toward the door. They did not want to leave their mother, and yet they were uncomfortable staying. Uncomfortable and helpless. Anna knew how they felt because she felt it too.

And we're all talking in jerks, she thought. They must all feel as she did. Her throat felt tight, too small for words to come through and sound normal.

"I'm starving," Fritz put in, sounding blessedly himself. "Make lots, Gretchen. How about eggs and sausages?"

"I'm making this for Mama, not you," Gretchen answered, but she gave him a grateful smile. He fell in beside her, obviously planning to persuade her further.

"Let me help," Rudi said suddenly.

He did not wait for his sister's reaction but strode out of the room ahead of them all. The three girls and his mother stared after him, their faces identical in their expression of astonishment. Not even trying, Rudi had managed to snap Mama out of her trance.

Papa chuckled, then sobered.

"Yes, let him help," he said. "He doesn't know what

15

to do with himself. After all, this is his first war. You know, Mama and I have already been through one. That's when we met."

Mama actually laughed. "You were so conceited in your uniform," she teased. "Such a strutting young peacock!"

"You couldn't resist me," Papa reminded her. "You weren't the only one either, you know, but I took pity on you."

Mama hit at him, lightly.

"Pity, was it?" she scoffed. "I remember you down on your knees—and all these children are the result of my feeling sorry for *you*?"

Reassured by the laughter, the two older girls left, Fritz following them. Anna, alone with her parents, watched them and had trouble believing her eyes and ears. She had seen first one and then the other in tears within the last hour, and now they were laughing, laughing about Papa going to war.

Anna felt her knees go weak. Papa at war!

"Papa," she croaked. "Papa . . ."

But when he turned, she could not go on. Miraculously, her father did not need her to put her terror into words.

"*Liebling*, I am forty-eight years old," he said, "and I have five children. They won't want me to fight."

"How can you even think such a thing!" Mama cried out. "This war is none of our concern. How could any of us fight against our homeland? Hitler is a madman!

16

When Germans see what he has led them into, they will recover their senses and it will be the end of him."

Papa got to his feet and reached down a strong hand to pull Mama to hers.

"Stop, Klara. Anna meant nothing."

As he led her away, leaving Anna without a backward glance of reassurance, Anna heard her mother say in a voice that shook, "Ernst, how can we find out if Tania is safe?"

Aunt Tania! Anna's eyes flew to a picture on the mantelpiece, taken long ago, on Uncle Karl's twenty-first birthday, in front of their home on Kastanien Allee in Hamburg. Uncle Karl stood terribly straight and looked proud of himself. He reminded Anna of Rudi, although in the picture Papa was the one who was Rudi's age. Aunt Tania, the youngest, had been just fifteen.

The sweet-faced girl in the photograph bore little resemblance to the aunt whom Anna remembered with affection, the aunt who had been so much a part of their lives before they left Frankfurt. That Aunt Tania was plump, quick to laugh, and kind like Papa. And, again like Papa, she had a special fondness for Anna, the Ugly Duckling among her brother's five children.

Mama had so often been impatient, even angry, with Anna in those days, and the little girl had known why. It was because she was clumsy while the others were graceful; she was slow while the others were swift; she was homely while the others were pleasing to the eye—

Rudi and Gretchen fair and tall like Papa, Frieda and Fritz dark and vivid like Mama herself. But Aunt Tania seemed not even to notice how awkward and plain her small niece was.

One day stood out in Anna's memory. They were playing tag and she had been It for a long time because everyone could run so much faster than she could. At last, trying extra hard to get to Gretchen, she had stumbled and fallen flat.

"Dummkopf," Rudi jeered, "there's nothing there to make anyone fall. You must have tripped over your own big feet."

She got up stoically. She had almost succeeded, by that time, in teaching herself not to cry because she sensed that Rudi liked to see her in tears. Seeing she seemed unhurt, the other three joined him in laughing at her.

"Couldn't catch a tortoise," Rudi went on. "Couldn't catch a snail. Silly baby. You're too slow to play our games. Go away."

"Shame!" Aunt Tania's voice cried out then.

How long she had been watching Anna never knew. But the look she gave the older children stopped their laughter as effectively as if she had doused them with ice water.

"Four against one!" she went on. "And you're all bigger. If I could, I would disown the pack of you. I want no cowardly bullies for nieces and nephews."

And without wasting another second on the rest, Aunt

Tania turned to Anna, gathered her up, and carried her, big as she was, into the house. She sat down in Mama's rocker, holding Anna close, and sang:

"Bei mein kindeles vigele,
Shteht a klor veis tzigele,
Dos tzigele iz getorn handlen.
Dos vet zein dein beruf,
Rozhinkes mit mandlen. . . ."

"Put her down, Tania," Mama had said sharply as the lullaby ended. "She's too big to be babied like that. She wasn't really hurt."

But Aunt Tania had paid no attention. This was the reason that Anna remembered this small incident for so long. She had sung the little Yiddish song through again.

It was then that Anna had put into actual words inside her head what had been only a vague, unformed longing before.

I wish Aunt Tania was my mother instead of Mama.

The next instant, she knew she wished no such thing. Not to belong to her own Papa! It could not be. Shocked at herself, she said in a small rough voice, "I'm all right. Let me go."

Mama had looked pleased. Anna, not wanting to see Aunt Tania's expression, ran from the room.

Aunt Tania was still in Germany. Did she already know that Germany and Canada were at war? Germany and

19

Britain anyway. Did that mean that they were on one side and Aunt Tania on the other?

We're Germans too, Anna thought, confused. Only we're against Hitler. Surely Aunt Tania is too.

The direction her thoughts were taking was growing more frightening every minute. Anna headed for the kitchen. At the sound of her step, Gretchen spoke without turning around.

"Frieda's gone up to get washed and comb her hair. Carry the rolls in, will you? Mama will be here any minute. I've made a really good breakfast to take her mind off the whole thing."

Anna, picking up the basket containing the hot rolls, paused to warn her sister.

"Mama's worried about Aunt Tania."

Gretchen's busy hands stilled for an instant. Then she went on stirring the hot chocolate to keep the milk from burning.

"That's nothing new really; there hasn't been a letter for months," she said. "But there's nothing you or I can do for Aunt Tania this minute, while we can make things easier for Mama, if we all try."

"And for Papa," Anna added, starting off for the dining room.

Gretchen's voice, pitched low so it wouldn't carry through the closed door to their parents' bedroom, came after her youngest sister.

"Of course, but things like this are always easier for men. Check the silverware."

Anna looked at the table. There were nasturtiums in a bowl in the center, their vivid gold and flame colors glowing as brightly as they had yesterday, before there had been a declaration of war. Sunlight glinted on knives, spoons, and forks, and on the blue china egg cups that Mama had been given when she married. Poland, Mr. Chamberlain, even Aunt Tania, seemed unreal, dim, and far off, nothing to do with life here in Toronto at all.

Gretchen was wrong though about Papa minding less. Anna knew. She had seen him weeping. That memory still made her feel cold and lonely way down inside, despite the sunlight and the nasturtiums.

3

THE FOLLOWING MORNING, Anna and Gretchen were cleaning the house. Although she was still feeling strange about the war, Anna had started to feel better about school. Her friend Isobel was going to take her there tomorrow, and she was coming today so they could talk about it. Isobel and Anna had been friends since they met in Sight-Saving Class. Just last year she had gone off to the same high school. She knew exactly how Anna would feel.

As she dusted, Anna kept looking out the window. Gretchen came to stand beside her and joined in looking out at the empty street.

"I thought Isobel wasn't coming till afternoon," she said, not needing to ask why Anna was keeping watch.

"She promised to come the minute she could get away, so there's a chance . . ." Anna began.

There was the sound of a car outside. Anna watched, but it passed the house without even slowing down.

Anna sighed, started listlessly to dust the thing nearest to her hand.

Papa's radio! As she ran her duster over it, she tried to believe that she was living in a country at war. She could not do it. Nothing in her life had changed to give the word "war" reality for her.

"Does it seem like wartime to you?" she asked.

Gretchen shook her head.

"You missed doing the ridge above the dial," she said. Anna, who only saw dust when it was an inch thick by Mama's standards, went back.

"Isobel wouldn't want to eat with us at noon anyway. We're having sauerkraut," Gretchen observed, making no move to proceed to an unmopped area.

"She says it isn't the taste she minds but the smell," Anna stopped dusting to reply. "It's the same with head cheese and tongue. Her parents like them, but Isobel won't even taste them because of their names."

"I can just picture Mama's expression if Isobel ever sat down at our table and held her nose while she ate," Gretchen said, grinning.

Anna burst out laughing. Then both girls heard steps

coming up from the basement and, without exchanging a word, they made duster and mop fly into action.

Having work to do did make the morning pass quickly though. Soon Anna was taking her place at the table, sniffing the aroma of sauerkraut and roast pork, which she loved even though Isobel did not. Still she wished the meal was over.

"How wonderful to be all together at home on a Monday noon!" Mama beamed around at the circle of faces.

Afraid her mother might notice her impatience to get dinner done with, Anna cast about for some way to change the subject.

"Where's Rudi?" she asked, seeing he was missing.

"He took sandwiches and went on a hike in High Park with his school friends and Mr. McNair," Mama said, her happiness dimming as she spoke. "I told him we'd like to have him with us, but he said they had planned this for a long time."

"Catch me ever going hiking with a teacher!" Fritz said, with an exaggerated shudder.

"Catch any teacher going hiking with you, you mean," Frieda said.

"Rudi's growing up, Klara," Papa said. "He'll be away more and more often. We'll just have to make up our minds to accept it."

Mama nodded in reluctant agreement, but Fritz laughed.

"He's not all *that* grown up," he said. "You should

have heard him talking in his sleep last night. He was talking German a lot of the time so I didn't get all of it. But he must have been playing something like tag in his dream. He counted up to ten and then he yelled out, 'I got you, Wolf. You're It.' And another time, he said, in a really furious voice, 'That's not fair, Helmut. It was my turn.' "

"How funny!" Gretchen said. "I haven't heard him mention Wolf or Helmut for years. I remember them, now I hear their names, but it all seems so long ago. . . . I don't remember ever dreaming about Frankfurt."

Papa looked as though he were about to say something about dreaming about Frankfurt himself, Anna guessed, but then he changed his mind.

"I never dream at all," Fritz said.

"When I wake up out of a really good dream, I make myself go back to sleep so I can finish it," Frieda told them. "Sometimes they're as good as a movie almost."

Anna was waiting for Mama to say she could begin to clear away the first course when her mother, blushing slightly, admitted that she, too, had dreamed she was back in Frankfurt.

"We were having dinner with the Jakobsohns," she said, "and just as I was about to start eating, I realized I had on that huge old flannel nightgown I used to wear when I was pregnant. And I said to you, Ernst, in as dignified a voice as I could manage, that I wanted you to take me home because I had a headache—and you turned around and stared at me and said, 'Do I know you?' as though you'd never set eyes on me before."

"Then what happened?" Anna demanded as the laughter around the table broke in on the story.

"I woke up," Mama said, "and I was greatly relieved to find myself safe in bed."

"With a man who didn't even know you," teased Gretchen.

"You and Anna may clear the table," Klara Solden said, pretending she was not amused.

Anna was on her way back from the kitchen when the doorbell rang. She almost dropped the bowl of fruit she was carrying.

"It's Isobel!" she cried. Dumping the dessert down in front of her mother, she ran to open the door.

But it wasn't Isobel; it was Mrs. Schumacher, Anna's teacher in Sight-Saving Class.

For one surprised moment, Anna stared, openmouthed. Then she came to her senses and beamed.

"Oh, I'm so glad to see you," she said, the glow in her face affirming her words. "It seems like years since you were last here. And Isobel's coming! She should be arriving any minute. She'll be so pleased when she finds you. Mama! It's Mrs. Schumacher."

Anna's parents came out to the hall to make her welcome.

"You got here at exactly the right minute," Mama said. "I baked a gugelhupf on Saturday night as a surprise for Isobel, and now you can share it."

"How's Franz?" Papa asked as they all moved back to the table. "It's been weeks since we've had a game of chess."

"He's fine," Mrs. Schumacher said, taking the chair Mama pulled forward for her. "More tired than usual, perhaps. The news, of course, and he's had a lot of pre-school medical examinations to do. Also, a youngster he's very fond of has polio. They still don't know whether she'll pull through. Even if she does, she'll be almost completely paralyzed. He's spent hours with her parents."

Everyone looked grave at this. A friend of Fritz's had died of polio two summers before. He had been perfectly well one day, and four days later he was dead.

Mrs. Schumacher's husband was a doctor. It was at one of those pre-school examinations that he discovered how poor Anna's eyesight was. Then he told her parents that even with the help of glasses, she would have much less than normal vision and she would have to go to a Sight-Saving Class. How angry she had been; how frightened! Yet over the years in that very class, Anna had changed from an unhappy outsider without friends into the person she was now.

What's so different? a voice inside her asked. You're just as scared now. You'll be an outsider again tomorrow.

"I thought Isobel would be here by now," Anna said then. "What time is it, Papa?"

"Nearly half past one," Papa said. "Don't worry, *Liebling*, she'll come in her own good time."

"I'm afraid she won't," Eileen Schumacher said. "That's

27

why I'm here. She telephoned our house a while ago. She had tried to get me all morning, she said, but I was over at the school, getting the classroom ready."

She paused for breath. Nobody spoke in the second of silence. Mrs. Schumacher went on.

"I'm afraid she's sick. She has a very sore throat and a fever. Franz says she must stay right in bed."

"But she's taking me to school tomorrow!" Anna said.

Only silence answered her.

"You mean she can't go out at all?" asked Anna, her voice thin.

"Not at all," Mrs. Schumacher said. "And there's something more. Perhaps we should go into the living room, Anna, and let the others finish eating while we talk."

Anna stood up like a puppet whose strings are jerked. She felt herself moving ahead of her guest into the next room. What else could there be? Isobel not coming with her . . . .

"Let's sit on the couch. Don't look like that, Anna. It's a disappointment but you'll weather it. Oh, Mr. Solden, I'm glad you came too."

Anna was dimly conscious of Papa sitting down in his usual chair. Mrs. Schumacher had taken her hand and was warming it between her own. Funny. She hadn't known her hands were cold. But suddenly they felt like ice.

"What is it? What's the matter?" Anna asked. The words came out in a whisper.

"There was a letter about Isobel's new school," Mrs.

Schumacher said, her voice calm and steady. "When the Browns moved last month, they didn't realize that they crossed the boundary between one school district and the next. Isobel won't be going to Davenport after all."

Mrs. Schumacher sounded sorry for Isobel. Anna glanced at her father. His face wore the same concerned expression. Didn't they realize what this meant to her, Anna? Didn't they care?

She saw, the next moment, that both of them were watching her with loving eyes. They were sorry for Isobel, but they were sorry for her, too.

She willed herself not to cry. They said nothing, letting her take her time, seeing that she wanted to speak. Finally, she managed to say, in a small pinched voice, "Can't I just stay on in the senior Sight-Saving Class with you? Please! I know you don't want me to but . . . but . . ."

She choked and had to stop.

"I would love to have you in my class, Anna, and you know it," Eileen Schumacher said. "You're a joy to teach. But you're ready to leave the nest. Right now, hundreds of students your age are facing the uncertainty of beginning high school tomorrow. If you go now, you'll be one of them and you'll learn to fit in along with everyone else. If you wait, the way Isobel did, till you've finished grade ten in a special class, the others will have already made their adjustment and their friendships too. If it hadn't been for your sisters, Isobel would have had a pretty lonely time last year."

"I don't feel ready to leave the nest," Anna said stubbornly, knowing the two of them were not going to let her win.

"Anna, we pushed you out years ago, not knowing you couldn't see, and you had a bad time in regular school in Germany," Papa said. "I'm sure that, deep down, you think it will be that way again. You do, don't you?"

She had never been able to lie to him. She nodded reluctantly.

"But you've come so far since then," Mrs. Schumacher said. "You've done nearly eight years' work in five! When you tried your entrance exams, you did exceptionally well and you were competing with pupils with normal sight."

"Not in math, I didn't," Anna muttered.

"Well, you passed anyway. Most people have one weak subject," her teacher said. "What's more, I think your main problem with math is sheer laziness. Anna, Anna, you're afraid because Isobel won't be there to go with you, but she couldn't have gone that far with you anyway. You have so much to learn about yourself, and you won't find it out while we keep you protected."

"I don't want to go alone!" Anna cried, making one last plea.

"Isobel told me to remind you that she isn't your only friend," Mrs. Schumacher said.

That made no sense. What other friend had she?

Then a new voice broke in.

"It's been fascinating eavesdropping from the hall,"

30

Gretchen said, "but I know my cue to enter when I hear it. What's Isobel got that I haven't, Anna Solden?"

Anna gaped at her.

Eileen Schumacher stood up and put one arm around Gretchen's shoulders.

"That's the last bit of Isobel's message," she said, looking down at Anna. "But I'm glad it's happened this way."

"Message?" Anna repeated, still at a loss. Could a sister be a friend?

"She said, 'Tell her to ask Gretchen. She's a tower of strength and she knows everything,'" Mrs. Schumacher quoted Isobel.

"I'm not so sure about that," Papa said slowly, smiling just a little.

"Well, Anna," Gretchen demanded, pretending not to notice her father. "Did you have something you wanted to ask me?"

Anna searched for words and a steady voice to go with them. "Will you take me to school tomorrow morning?" she got out, finally. "Please."

"I've given it due consideration," her sister said, "and the answer's yes."

Relief opened inside Anna like the petals of a flower unfurling.

"Poor Isobel," she said, suddenly able to think beyond her own fear.

"Isobel?" Gretchen echoed, feeling sorry for Isobel herself but wondering precisely why Anna was.

31

"To be sick in bed," Anna said, "and to be an only child."

As Mrs. Schumacher was going out the door, she slipped an envelope into Anna's hand.

"Isobel gave me this," she said. "She said to tell you to read it when you were by yourself. And Anna, if ever you need me, just come. I'll do my best to help."

"Thank you," Anna said, knowing that it was a real promise.

She took the letter up to her alcove as soon as she'd waved good-bye.

Dear Anna,

Mrs. Schumacher will get you to start tomorrow, I know, so I won't go on about that. I just have one thing I want to say. It's important, so pay attention and don't waste time getting mad. Remember that I always know best.

At the end of that sentence she had drawn a small smiling face.

Tomorrow do NOT act the way you did when you first came to the Sight-Saving Class, stiff and hard to talk to and never smiling. We knew you were just scared but high school kids aren't that smart.

Smile! Don't wait for one of them to smile first either. Smile as though they've already smiled and you're smiling back. If one ignores you, cross her off and smile at others till you find a friend. You can do it.

Good luck! Phone me tomorrow night and tell me what happens.

Love,
Isobel

4

THE NEXT MORNING, Anna got dressed with great care. Gretchen had inspected her outfit the night before and approved. She put on a white blouse, a gray pleated skirt, white ankle socks, and the sturdy oxfords that Mama insisted on, even though they were expensive and the girls hated them. She undid her hair, plaited in two pigtails for the night, and brushed it hard, hoping it would somehow change from a dull brown to a brown with golden glints. She then rebraided it, crossing the braids over the top of her head, toward the front, so they would look like a crown. At least, that was what Mama claimed. To Anna, they looked ugly, with wisps slipping loose no matter how tightly she did the braids and regardless of how many bobby pins she used to try to hold them in place. It was impossible hair.

She dawdled till the other girls went down, calling to her to hurry. Then, picking up the powder-blue cardigan Papa had given her for her birthday, she went in to the full-length mirror that stood in her sister's room. She did not want to look because she knew it would be anything but encouraging, but somehow she could not go off to face strangers without checking her appearance.

She saw her usual roundish solemn face, her thick glasses that made her blue-gray eyes look bigger but not more beautiful, her crown of braids, her neat appearance. One thing helped. The sweater made her eyes look more blue than gray. She had been very careful with the sweater, wearing it only on very special occasions, and it looked brand-new.

"It's lovely," Gretchen had said the night before, stroking it. "I just hope it's not too warm for you to wear it."

"If it is, I'll carry it over my arm in case it turns cool later," Anna said, having already made up her mind about that.

If only I were prettier, she thought, staring at herself. What I look is dull.

Then she thought of Isobel's letter. She smiled at herself. Isobel was absolutely right. The smile did make a difference. She really must remember to smile the way she had been told.

35

When she went down to breakfast, Mama took one look at her and disappeared into her bedroom. A moment later, she was back with a small velvet box. Anna, recognizing it, held her breath. It was Mama's cameo, an ivory face set in an oval of Wedgwood blue. Mama took it from its box and tipping up Anna's chin, pinned it at the neck of her blouse.

"What did you do to deserve that, Anna?" Frieda demanded, pretending to be overcome by envy.

"It's exactly right," Gretchen said. "I tried to think of something last night but I had nothing that would do. You're a genius, Mama."

Mama smiled and kissed Anna on the top of her head, much to everyone's amazement.

"It is a special moment," she said sentimentally. "My baby is growing up."

She pulled a handkerchief out of her apron pocket, blew her nose briskly, and proceeded in her usual half-scolding voice, "Don't just sit, Anna. Eat. You can't begin high school on an empty stomach."

But Anna had trouble eating enough to satisfy her mother. She sipped at her hot chocolate instead. It slid down when nothing else would.

"Come on, Anna," Gretchen said at last. "I know, Mama. She hasn't eaten enough to keep a bird alive. But she'll eat plenty when she comes home. If I'm to get her registered before the assembly starts, we have to leave right this minute."

Mama came to the door to watch them set out.

"Be careful crossing the streets on your way home, *Liebling*," she called after them.

On your way home. Magic words. Anna turned and waved wildly.

"Good-bye, Mama," she called. "Thank you for lending me your brooch. Good-bye!"

"You're only going half a mile and you'll be back at noon," Gretchen said.

"By noon?"

"Sure. This morning there's an assembly first thing. Then there's your regular schedule of classes except they're cut short. Just long enough for you to find out each teacher's name, see where all the rooms you have to go to are, fill in seating plans, and find out what books you need to buy. Nobody should assign homework even, but somebody always does."

Noon, Anna thought. However awful it was, it would all be over within three and a half hours.

She hurried to keep up. As they neared the school, Gretchen stopped to greet several friends, explaining each time that she was getting Anna registered and she'd see them later. Anna wanted to thank her sister, but the right moment never seemed to come. Then they were there.

"We go this way, Anna," Gretchen said. "Hold on to my arm or I might lose you in the crowd."

Anna clutched her older sister's elbow with her right hand. Over her other arm, she carried the blue sweater.

Now she hugged it close to herself for comfort and, tugged along by Gretchen, entered Davenport Collegiate for the first time.

Other girls and boys pushed in behind her, blocking the exit. She thought, It's a trap. And I'm caught.

"Anna, don't hold on *that* tight. You're breaking my arm," Gretchen said. Then she turned her head and looked down at Anna's face.

"Don't worry so," she said gently. "I won't leave you. And anyway, it's not forever."

They were in the middle of a pushing mob. Anna would have had to shout to make Gretchen hear. She had only half heard Gretchen, half read the words on her lips. But she fought down the panic she knew her sister had sensed. She did not think she could smile, though.

Then a boy, going by them, said, "Welcome back to the dungeon, Gret."

And Gretchen laughed.

"Hi, Barry," she said.

If Gretchen could laugh at dungeon!

Anna smiled. It was a shaky smile. But it was a smile. Then, gathering courage from her own effort to be brave, she leaned close to her big sister and did shout, loudly enough to be heard.

"Lead on," she said. "Show me the way to my cell."

"You start here, at the warden's office," Gretchen shouted back.

The woman behind the desk had enrolled a lot of new

students already that morning. She scarcely glanced up as Anna, Gretchen right behind her, came to a halt before her desk.

"Grade Nine?" she asked and then, without looking up to catch Anna's nod, went on as though she already knew. "Your name?"

"Anna Solden," Anna said, trying hard to speak in a clear firm voice that would not betray to this indifferent woman the rapid pounding of her heart, the queasy feeling in her stomach, and the trembling of her knees. She was amazed to hear her voice sounding exactly the way she intended it to!

"Solden . . . Solden . . . Here it is. Anna Elisabeth. Right?"

This time, the woman did look up, so Anna simply nodded again. No use taking chances on her voice staying calm.

"Let's see. You're in Mr. Lloyd's homeroom. 9E. It's on this same floor. Turn left after you leave here and . . ."

"I know the way," Gretchen said. "I'll show her. She's my sister."

The woman looked up again, her tiredness and her efficiency both vanishing for a moment, and smiled at Gretchen.

"Nice to see you back," she said. "I should have guessed. Have you any more Soldens at home?"

"She's the last," Gretchen told her. "Five more years and you'll be rid of all of us."

"I don't expect to last out the day, let alone five years, but I'd better keep at it. Next, please."

As the girls left, Anna heard a voice saying, "Maggie de Vries."

Maggie didn't sound scared at all.

But then, neither did I, Anna told herself.

Then she and Gretchen were making their way down the crowded hall to find 9E.

Gretchen pulled Anna off to one side and stopped walking.

"Who did she say the teacher was?" Anna asked, taking advantage of the slight lessening of noise.

"Mr. Lloyd," Gretchen said, her face close to Anna's. "That's what I want to warn you about. Mr. Lloyd's . . ."

"The meanest man alive," Anna filled in.

"How did you know?"

"I remember somebody saying it last year. Fritz maybe. But I'd forgotten till you said his name in that loathing kind of way," Anna explained. She felt a tightening in her chest. "Is he really?"

"Yes. You could have heard any of us saying it. We've been saying it every day for years. Mr. Lloyd is mean and he's a rotten teacher and he's unfair. He has teacher's pets too. But you won't be one."

Anna did not think she would ever be a teacher's pet, although she knew Mrs. Schumacher had liked her a lot. She hurriedly pushed the thought of Mrs. Schumacher out of her mind.

"He's taught all the rest of us," Gretchen explained,

"and he hasn't liked one. When he hears the name Solden, he'll have it in for you right away."

"But what did you all do?" Anna asked, incredulous. She had always thought of her brothers and sisters, with the possible exception of Fritz, as being model students.

"He didn't mind me too much," Gretchen admitted. "Rudi was the one who really drove him mad."

"Rudi!" Anna echoed, astonished. Rudi, she thought for sure, was teacher's pet every time.

"Mr. Lloyd had to teach this one class of history. The teacher who was supposed to take it died or something. I don't know. Anyway, he didn't know his history that well and Rudi was smarter than he was and . . ."

Anna didn't need to have it explained any further. She could just hear Rudi correcting the teacher. She felt a momentary stab of pity for this Mr. Lloyd.

"What I'm trying to say is—don't make him notice you, Anna. Don't ask him any questions and just—be careful, that's all. If only he wasn't your homeroom teacher! We'd better get moving. I just had to warn you so if he says anything nasty, you'll be prepared."

They went on, hurrying now.

"Here's the door," Gretchen announced suddenly. "Now, just remember how we got here and you'll be able to find it again after the assembly."

Anna stared at her sister dumbly. She had simply followed along. How could she have paid attention with Mr. Lloyd to think about?

"Anna, *look* at the door so you'll recognize it," Gretchen

41

ordered, impatience creeping into her voice for the first time. Anna understood. Gretchen wanted to get back to her friends. She looked, obediently, at the classroom door. Then she glanced down the hall in first one direction and then the other. As far as she could see, identical doors lined the hallway.

"It says MR. LLOYD 9E right there on the card," Gretchen pointed out, the impatience more noticeable.

Anna did see that there was a small card fitted into a brass slot on the door, but she saw nothing written on it. She moved closer. Still no words were visible. Just a grayish blur where the words must be. She would have to go up on tiptoe and put her nose right against it to be sure. Still, she guessed she could, if she really had to.

"Yes, I see," she murmured, looking down.

And, doing so, she discovered to her relief and delight a big, crooked scratch farther down, going right across the varnish. It looked as though somebody had done it on purpose with the point of a compass maybe. But how it got there didn't matter.

"I'll recognize it," she said, lifting her head and facing Gretchen with assurance.

"Good. I'll take you to the gym where we have assembly. Watch how we go and you'll be able to get back here. If you think you can't, I could meet you after. My class sits near the back and yours sits right up in the front rows. Do you think you can find the way again?"

Anna longed to say no, but she could tell Gretchen

42

was hoping she wouldn't. She rubbed her sweaty palms on her skirt and took a deep breath.

"I'll be okay," she said.

"It isn't hard really," Gretchen said, sounding pleased. They came to the gym. She led Anna up to the front.

"There's where you sit."

She pointed to four empty chairs in the first row. Anna started toward them, forcing herself to move resolutely. Then she stopped and turned back. Gretchen was waiting, making sure she made it safely.

"Thanks a lot, Gretchen," she said, not sure the words would carry over the buzz of talk in the auditorium. Gretchen smiled and wiggled her thumb up and down in the family good-luck sign. When Anna reached the chairs, two were still vacant. She sat down on the nearest one quickly before anybody else could take it. She looked back to where Gretchen had been standing, but her sister was gone.

Anna felt all her courage suddenly drain away, as though she had pulled out a plug in a basin. She could not put the plug back in, but she could sit here and pretend she was no different from all the other students. She might not feel brave, but she could keep herself from crying or from shaking so everyone could see. So what if she looked unfriendly! She sat, stiff as a stone statue, and waited.

A teacher walked across the stage and sat down at the piano. Anna automatically rose with everyone else and stood at attention. She listened to the others singing "God Save the King." All around her, kids were joining right in, even though they must be newcomers too, by what Gretchen had said. Anna moved her mouth and hoped she looked as though she were singing as loudly as any of them.

At the end, she almost sat down. Some of the other new students did sit, but scrambled up again when they saw the older students still on their feet.

A tall boy came to the microphone. Anna could see he had something in his hand. A slip of paper? He led them in the Lord's Prayer. Anna, saying the words inside her head, didn't close her eyes. She watched the boy. She thought he was reading the words. Didn't he know them? He must. But leading everyone must make him nervous, though he looked at least as old as Gretchen. Anna felt slightly better about her own fears. Nearing the finish of the prayer, she did murmur one line aloud, changing it to a personal plea: "Deliver me from evil."

The next moment, they were all sitting down. The boy introduced himself. He was last-year's Student Council president. Anna realized suddenly that she had a slight advantage over some of the other beginners. She had been listening to her brothers and sisters talk about this school for years. She was glad that the twins and Gretchen were somewhere in this very same hall. Even without Isobel, she had protectors.

"And now I'll turn things over to our principal, Mr. Appleby," the boy said.

The students cheered, clapped, stamped their feet. One or two even whistled.

They must really like him, Anna thought.

She wished she had a watch. How much of the morning was over? That was what she wanted to know. Not much, she decided. Noon seemed light-years away. If she couldn't find Mr. Lloyd's room, what would she do? If she just stood there, till everyone else went away, someone would be sure to see her and come to ask why she wasn't at a class and then . . .

The crowd burst out laughing. Mr. Appleby must have told a joke. She tuned in for a moment. He was talking about working hard. She let her thoughts drift again. Then, a familiar name made her really pay attention.

". . . Rudi Solden, who wrote his Departmentals last June and got perfect marks in advance chemistry and trigonometry. He also came very close to one hundred percent in advanced physics. Rudi should be an inspiration to all of you. He came to Canada just five years ago, speaking very little English. But it improved by leaps and bounds, and his schoolwork was never less than excellent. We were delighted when he was awarded the McNab Memorial Scholarship. We know he'll go on to win more honors at the University of Toronto in his chosen course of math, physics, and chemistry. But we'll always be proud to know that he is a graduate of this school. I see other Soldens looking up at me. Gretchen and Frieda, each in her own way, have contributed much to D.C.V.I. Fritz, now, would do well to ponder on his brother's academic success and do a little more home-work, although what we'd do without him on the bas-ketball court, I don't know. Miss Gregory, in the office, told me just before I came out here that the last of the Soldens is beginning school here this morning."

There was a pause while his eyes swept the front rows. Anna went scarlet but sat absolutely still, hoping he would not notice her. Their eyes met, locked for an instant during which Anna knew she had been recognized, and then he looked past her.

How had he known her? For she was certain he had. She didn't look a bit like the others. Maybe Miss Gregory had told him that too and her telltale blush had told him the rest.

"Wherever you are sitting, Anna," he said smoothly, not looking in her direction again, "remember that I'm here to help you in any way I can. That goes for every new student beginning here this morning. It's a big school and I'm sure most of you have a bit of a hollow, lost feeling right this minute, but it'll be all right soon. You'll see."

Behind Anna, someone applauded loudly. Mr. Appleby looked to see who it was and chuckled.

"Thank you, Boris," he said. "We couldn't have a better recommendation."

"You're quite welcome, sir," a boy's voice replied.

Anna straightened at the sound of it. So it was *that* Boris! He was a friend of Fritz's. He had come over from

England halfway through the school year, had had trouble adjusting, and had failed. The next year, he had failed again, through sheer lack of work. Last year, when Fritz got to know him, he had settled down and headed the class. He'd set Fritz enough of a good example so that Fritz, too, had passed respectably. Boris must really like and trust Mr. Appleby to have had nerve enough to clap that way. And Mr. Appleby's voice, even while it teased a little, had made clear his liking for Boris, too.

The principal went on for another couple of minutes. Anna spent the time wondering why he had said so much about her family. Somehow she had received an impression that he had done it on purpose. But why?

It was over. Everyone was standing up. Anna got up too, copying the rest. Boys and girls all around her set off with what looked like boundless confidence to their various homerooms. She herself stood still. Which direction was it? What if she couldn't . . . ?

Then Gretchen's directions came back to her. She walked over to the hall, turned right—she was pretty sure this was the way they had come—and walked slowly, very slowly, down the next long hallway, her eyes searching each door as she passed it, searching but not at all sure . . .

Then she saw it. The door, standing open but with the jagged scratch across it. 9E!

"I did it!" Anna said out loud. She looked around.

Nobody seemed to have heard her. Nobody was noticing her at all, except that she was standing still and people wanted to get past. She lifted her chin, reached up and touched Mama's cameo to give herself added courage, and, pretending she knew exactly what to do next, she walked into Mr. Lloyd's homeroom.

5

ANNA WOULD HAVE HESITATED just inside the door, hoping to get her bearings, but a thrust of bodies behind her sent her forward and she was standing by the teacher's desk before she could come to a halt. She glanced at the straight chair behind it and then, doing her best to appear casual, looked around the rapidly filling room. As far as she could tell, Mr. Lloyd had not yet arrived. Some of the people clustered in the back corner by the windows were tall. But even though she could not see them distinctly, Anna knew that the teacher was not among them. Everyone was too relaxed. All around her she could hear bits of conversation, which would not be taking place with such a teacher as Mr. Lloyd within earshot.

"Are you going to try out for the rugby team?"

"Mother wanted me to wear a summer dress when I'd made her buy me this skirt especially. . . ."

"My cousin warned me about this teacher. . . ."

"Are you going to see *The Wizard of Oz*?"

"Let's sit near the back."

The last remark told Anna what to do next. Find a desk for herself. Even in a front seat, she would not be able to read what was written on the board unless the teacher had really large writing, but at least she would have a better idea of what was going on. Here the desks were all nailed to the floor in straight rows. In the Sight-Saving Class, they had separate desks that could be moved up till they even touched the board if necessary. And there had been much brighter overhead lights. And the boards had been green instead of slate colored. And the chalk had been fat and yellow instead of skinny and . . .

Realizing that she was standing still, lost in a flood of memory, Anna hurried to move toward the front desk right in the center.

Nobody else would want it. She slid into the seat and sighed with relief. Now she didn't look different if anybody was looking. Her common sense told her nobody was. But she seemed to feel all eyes staring at her, everybody thinking things like What's wrong with that girl in the funny-looking glasses? Gee, she looked dumb, just standing there!

Well, she wasn't just standing there any longer. She was placing her sweater on the seat beside her, arranging the battered, two-ring zippered notebook Gretchen had given her in the exact center of the desk, taking out her new fountain pen and trying it out on a bit of paper to make sure it had enough ink in it. Having filled it just the night before, she knew it had, but it looked like a normal thing to be doing, she thought.

"Hey, don't sit there, kid," a boy's voice said.

Anna jumped guiltily and glanced up, ready to look away quickly if he were not actually speaking to her. He was though. He towered above her, his hair as fair as Rudi's, his face kind. He didn't know her but he was taking the trouble to try to help her as though they were friends.

"My brother had Leadhead two years ago and he told me that he eats the kids alive who sit up front."

"But . . . I chose this place on purpose," Anna said. "I can't see very . . ."

The boy, looking over her head, did not let her finish. His voice dropped to a whisper.

"Here he comes. Don't say I didn't warn you!"

He was gone, heading for the back row, Anna was sure. Had he heard her attempt to explain?

Then she took in what he had said and turned, her whole body tensing, to see the man Fritz called "the meanest man alive." She expected some kind of ogre. Mr. Lloyd looked too ordinary to be as bad as they said. As he crossed the room to his desk, students filled in the last seats. Since there were no extra places, Anna was not the only one in the front row.

Mr. Lloyd was not remotely like Papa. He had no laughter lines around his eyes. Anna could not usually have seen that, but he leaned across his desk to pick up a long ruler and she was only about a foot and a half away from him. What hair he had was reddish. He wore glasses with steel rims that glittered. His mouth looked as though he were biting his lips. But he was not tall. He looked not much taller than Mama. Anna wondered where she had received the impression that he was a giant.

Then he spoke and she knew. He roared exactly like a giant. And nobody had done anything yet to make him angry.

"Silence at once! This is a classroom, not a monkey house. Stop that jabbering this instant!" He banged on his desk with the heavy ruler.

Anna felt herself jump at the unexpected loudness.

"I'm warning you right now that I want no trouble from you. And I mean it! You'd better learn, and learn fast, that when I say 'Silence' I don't want to hear so much as one whisper. Or a page turning. Or any sound at all! Is that quite clear?"

Nobody moved. Were they supposed to answer somehow? Not a soul dared chance it.

"If there's anyone here who thinks he can show off and make mischief in this classroom, he'd better think again, for I can tell you right now that I'm more than a match for him. Is that understood?"

Finally, the tension told. One boy, unable to help himself, snickered nervously. Mr. Lloyd was around the desk and down the aisle like a shot, banging into Anna's elbow as he passed. He grabbed the now completely sober boy by the shoulder and jerked him out of his seat.

"Stand up and face me," he shouted.

Anna peered back over her shoulder, ready to turn in a flash if the teacher should start to look in her direction. The poor boy stood, brick red to his ears, head hanging, a good six inches taller than the man glaring up at him.

"I'll have an apology out of you this minute or you'll go to see the principal," Mr. Lloyd threatened.

Anna had once seen a turkey gobbler, fussing away noisily over nothing, puffed up to twice his size and looking silly. She thought of him suddenly, and speedily pushed the picture out of her head, in case somehow Mr. Lloyd could read minds.

Why doesn't the boy just say he'd rather go to see Mr. Appleby? she wondered, remembering how kind the principal had sounded when he spoke to those in Grade Nine. But she knew. To say such a thing would mean . . . Anna could not think of anything short of murder on the spot.

"I'm sorry," the boy mumbled.

"I'm sorry, *sir*!"

"I'm sorry, sir," the boy repeated, keeping his voice expressionless, his face blank.

The teacher shoved him back toward his seat and stamped back up the aisle.

He's got us scared the way he wants, but nobody's ever going to like him, Anna thought, keeping her eyes down.

Without another word, Mr. Lloyd opened the register and began to take roll call. There was no need to instruct them how to answer when he called their names.

"Barbara Abbott."

"Present, sir."

"Mark Ayre."

"Present, sir."

Anna listened as the names went by. None meant anything to her.

"Simon Dangerfield."

"Present, sir."

"Margaret de Vries."

"Present, sir. But I'm called Maggie."

Mr. Lloyd lowered the book and stared over Anna's head at the girl who had spoken out of turn.

"Your name is Margaret, Miss de Vries, is it not?"

"Yes, but . . ."

"There will be no use of nicknames in this class," Mr. Lloyd told her, and went on.

Anna wished she dared look around and see the girl who had had courage enough almost to argue. She suddenly remembered hearing Maggie's voice before, as she and Gretchen were leaving the office. So there was a name she knew.

Thank goodness they don't call me Annie, she thought.

They were nearing the S's now. But she knew exactly

54

what to do, after listening to so many others. Nothing could go wrong. Even if he did remember her brothers and sisters, he would not say anything about them at this point, surely.

"Carl Schmidt."

"Present, sir."

"Anna Solden."

"Present, sir."

Anna relaxed and waited for the next name to be called. Mr. Lloyd did not go on.

"Schmidt and Solden," he said slowly. "Where was your father born, Schmidt?"

"Kitchener, Ontario, sir," Carl answered.

Anna had been to Kitchener just last spring to visit friends of the Schumachers. Many German people had settled there on coming to Canada. She remembered Dr. Schumacher telling Papa that the city had been called Berlin, after the city in Germany, until the 1914–1918 war.

"And your mother?"

There was a tiny pause as though maybe the boy had not heard the question.

"In Munich," Carl said, dropping the "sir."

Anna waited for Mr. Lloyd to yell at the boy but he was on another track and did not even notice.

"In Germany. Just as I thought," he said, his voice ominous though the words sounded harmless enough. "And you, Miss Solden? Where are your parents from?"

Unsure of what he was after but frightened all the same, Anna lapsed into the accent of her childhood.

"Papa came from Hamburg and Mama from Frankfurt, but we lived in Frankfurt until we came to Canada," she said.

Only after it was out did she realize she had said more than she needed to say and played right into his hands.

"Well, well," Mr. Lloyd said, "so you really are a German yourself, Miss Solden? Are you proud of your Fatherland?"

Anna stared at him, feeling like a trapped bird. What did he want from her? How could she answer? This was a thousand times worse than having him ask if she was Rudi's sister.

"Miss Solden, you are German, are you not?"

"*I* am, sir," a quick, breathless voice said, breaking the tension for a second and then adding to it. "I'm a real German. Well . . . half."

"What do you mean? Who . . . ?"

"I'm Paula Kirsch. Mother's Scottish but my father's parents were German and, believe it or not, I was actually born in Austria in Brauman am Inn, the exact place where Herr Schicklgruber came from. He calls himself Adolf Hitler now. Is this a history lesson, sir?"

Anna could not believe her ears. Mr. Lloyd looked as if he might literally explode. She could see veins standing out on his forehead. She had never felt more afraid. How did that girl dare talk back to him like that?

"Aren't you going to finish taking the roll?" came another voice, a boy's this time. It sounded like the boy who had warned her not to sit up front. "My name's Weber, sir. You haven't got to me yet."

Mr. Lloyd snatched up the book from the desk where he had laid it after calling out Anna's name. The book shook in his hands.

He can't be afraid of us! Anna thought, not believing her eyes.

"Susan Sowerby," the teacher got out.

"Present, sir."

"Martin Tait."

"Present, sir."

The crisis was over.

There were only a few minutes left in which to do several important things. Mr. Lloyd ordered them to copy down the morning's schedule and the name of the textbook from the board. Anna strained but could not make out the words. The teacher's writing was as small and crabbed as he was himself. She looked across at a girl who had answered to the name of Nancy French. Nancy probably would not mind letting her copy if she asked. Then, thinking of what might happen if she were caught whispering even so innocent a request, Anna knew she could not do it.

"Never be afraid to explain and ask for help," Papa always said.

But Papa had not met Mr. Lloyd.

And he taught them geography first thing Monday and Wednesday mornings. Well, at least that way, it would be done with early in the day!

At last! The bell! They sprang to their feet. Mr. Lloyd made them all sit down again and get up properly, row by row, filing in order out the door.

Anna was one of the first ones out. She was right behind Nancy French. Nancy was wearing a cherry-red blouse, so she was easy to follow. Even though they were walking in line, as they had been instructed, Anna had a feeling that, if she took her eyes off that bright blouse, she might easily drift into the wrong lineup in the crowded hall.

While she concentrated, though, she heard bits of indignant conversation.

"Who does he think he is—God Almighty?"

"I was petrified!"

"I thought he'd have a heart attack when Paula talked back!"

"To think I looked forward to coming to high school!"

Then Nancy French turned her head and spoke directly to Anna. "I think he ought to be reported—or something. The way he yelled at Dave!"

"He's terrifying," Anna said, still shaking somewhere inside.

"He didn't scare me," Nancy said. "Not even Germans frighten me."

She watched Anna.

Like a cat watching a mouse, Anna thought, but I'm no mouse.

She was pleased to hear the calm in her own voice as she answered.

"That's nice."

Their row had to stop to let another line pass. Nancy, not looking where she was going, bumped into the girl in front of her.

"Watch out!" the girl snapped.

"So sorry," Nancy said, not sounding sorry at all.

She paid no more attention to Anna.

If you expect me to smile at *her*, forget it, Anna told Isobel inside her head.

The Latin teacher was an elderly lady with a firm cool voice. She made no mention of the war, not Hitler's war. She did tell them they would begin studying Caesar's wars before Christmas.

"You will find them extremely interesting," Miss Ogilvie said.

Anna decided she was going to like Latin.

Miss Raymond, who was to teach them French, sounded unsure of herself but she admitted openly that it was her first day of teaching. The class whispered but not too much. She was pretty enough to make them show mercy to her, this time at least.

English came next. Miss Sutcliff was wonderful. She had them skip making a seating plan so she could share a poem with them. When she started to read it aloud,

59

Anna was delighted to find it was a poem Papa had given her to memorize.

> *"I never saw a moor.*
> *I never saw the sea,*
> *Yet know I how the heather looks*
> *And what a wave must be.*
>
> *"I never spoke with God*
> *Nor visited in Heaven,*
> *Yet certain am I of the spot*
> *As though the chart were given.*

"What Emily Dickinson is saying in this poem is one of the chief reasons why we study English literature," Miss Sutcliff said. "Think about it. We'll discuss it tomorrow."

She then read aloud the list of books they would need. Anna gave her credit for being considerate even though the teacher had no idea yet that she had a pupil who could not read what was written on the board.

Great Expectations, *A Midsummer Night's Dream*, a book of poems, one of Greek and Roman myths, and a final one called *Shorter Essays*.

Great expectations! Anna thought, as she got up to go. That's exactly the way I feel about English class. And we have it every day.

In the hall, following Nancy French again, Anna tried to figure out what the teacher meant about the poem containing a reason for studying literature. Was it because, through reading, you could go places you couldn't travel to any other way? She, too, knew how the heather looked because of reading *The Secret Garden*. Books made the whole world yours, if you read enough. That must be it.

Suddenly, a big boy, hurrying to somewhere, cut right in front of her through the line of students. Startled, she glanced after him. When she turned back in search of Nancy, the girl in the red blouse was nowhere in sight. There was no one else Anna recognized. All around her other students marched briskly by, clearly knowing exactly where they were going. Then the crowd thinned as boys and girls disappeared into classrooms. Up and down the halls, brown doors closed, shutting her outside.

Anna did not just stand there. She made herself walk ahead, turn right where she thought Nancy must have . . . might have gone, and then she stopped beside the first door. It wasn't quite closed. If it was the right one, she would only be seconds behind the rest of her class. But how would she know? And even if it was the right room, would she be able to see an empty desk? Somehow, it was harder to see clearly when she was frightened and embarrassed. But she had to do something!

If only she'd copied that schedule. . . .

Knowing it would be no help, she opened her notebook and looked at the room plan. The print was pale purple and indecipherable.

The card on the door! Nobody would know if she

looked right up close. She tried to make it out. It was smudged, but did it say . . .

Accidentally, she pushed against the door and it slammed shut. She gasped and backed up. Then she heard a man's voice say, "Would one of you open that door? It's stuffy in here. They've just painted the sills and I can't open the windows."

Anna put out her hand and opened the door herself. It was better than having someone catch her skulking outside. The man's voice had sounded friendly.

Edging in, she blinked at the brightness of the room. If only she could spot Nancy!

"Can I help you?" the teacher asked.

"Please, I'm lost," Anna said. "I'm looking for class 9E."

Before he could answer, she saw Nancy French's blouse. And Nancy herself looking miraculously familiar.

Anna stepped forward and smiled.

"Hi, Nancy," she said.

Nancy just looked at her.

Certain it was Nancy, but unnerved by her silence and not seeing an empty desk anywhere, Anna stopped, not knowing what to do next.

Maybe it wasn't Nancy. She had made mistakes before.

Then another girl stood up and beckoned.

"We're 9E. You're not lost," the girl said. "You're supposed to be right here. Come sit by me."

Anna went, keeping her eyes wide open so no tears

would spill over and disgrace her. She sat down in the desk next to her rescuer.

"I'm Maggie de Vries," the girl said softly from across the aisle. "You're Anna Solden. I remember you because you registered just before I did and because . . ."

She stopped, flushing.

"Because of Mr. Lloyd," Anna finished for her.

"He was awful!" Maggie said. "How come you got lost?"

"I can't see very well," Anna began to explain. "I was following Nancy . . . Who is he? Where are we?"

"Mr. McNair. Algebra."

"Stop chattering, you two," Mr. McNair said. "Copy down the name of the book from the board. I'll expect every one of you to have that book with you tomorrow morning. The book and whatever brains you happen to possess. You'll need them in this class."

Mr. McNair was the teacher who had befriended Rudi, suggesting he try for the scholarship and giving him extra tutoring. There was a smile in his voice now, but Anna felt defeat. Mathematics was her worst subject.

"Do you need help?" Maggie whispered, as though she had not been told to hush. Anna nodded. This desk was halfway back, and Mr. McNair's writing looked hopeless. She couldn't see it at all from here.

Maggie worked busily for an instant and then passed a page across to Anna. The name of the text had been printed in big careful letters. Anna, too pleased to do anything but smile, wrote it in her own notebook.

As she did, she thought briefly of Nancy's unfriendly face. Then she remembered Mr. McNair saying, "Stop chattering, you two." That made Maggie and her sound as though they were forever talking, like old friends.

And what were the words Maggie had said, the words that had reached out to her, drawn her to safety, and given her a feeling of belonging?

"You're not lost. You're supposed to be right here. Come sit by me."

Anna thought that, for the rest of her life, she would remember Maggie saying those words. Compared to their warmth, being lost seemed not to matter at all.

6

WHEN THEY STOOD UP to go to the next class, Maggie reached across the aisle and touched Anna's arm.

"You stick with us," she said, as Anna looked up. "It must have been awful walking in all by yourself like that."

"It was," Anna said simply.

"Paula and I . . . Here's Paula," Maggie said, turning to a dark-haired girl across the aisle on the opposite side of her. "Paula, this is—"

"I know. Hi," said Paula.

"She's Paula Kirsch, the famous Austrian," Maggie said with a grin.

"Thank you," Anna said, "for making him stop."

Paula shrugged. "I hate a bully," she said.

"Were you really born where you said?" Anna asked. It didn't seem possible.

"I sure was. My parents were visiting relatives of Dad's and I surprised them by arriving a month ahead of when I was expected. Mother hasn't forgiven me yet. I was supposed to be born in Glasgow, where her mother lives."

"I don't know how you dared, all the same," Anna said.

"She beat up on boys all through public school, whenever she caught them picking on smaller kids," Maggie said. "Every boy I know is scared to death of her."

By now, they were in line and leaving the room. Mr. McNair stopped them momentarily.

"So you're Rudi's sister," he said.

Anna nodded.

"It should be a pleasure having you in the class," Mr. McNair said. "Rudi is the finest student of mathematics I have ever taught."

Should she warn him that what was true of Rudi was far from true of his youngest sister? He would find out soon enough.

"Thank you. I'll tell him," she surprised herself by saying.

She was so used to being tongue-tied or stammering at moments like that. Maybe the fact that she was in high school had suddenly made her more mature.

"Maggie! Paula! Wait up!"

A tall pretty redhead came racing up to them.

"I wondered where you'd disappeared to," Maggie said, not sounding terribly excited at the sight of her.

"I saw Mike Jelinek back there and I just stopped to ask him if he was going out for the rugby team. He's a bit clumsy but he's so strong!"

"I should have guessed," Maggie said. "Get in line, Suzy, and walk fast. We're miles behind."

"What's the next class?" Paula asked, over her shoulder.

"Home Ec," Maggie said. "That's why the boys went off in a different direction. I know the Home Ec room's along here someplace."

Anna, placed between Paula and Maggie, felt better than she had all morning. There was something trustworthy about Maggie. Something kind. And Paula must be as brave as a lion. Beating up boys!

"Here," Maggie said, and the four girls scurried through the door.

The Home Ec teacher was a short cushiony woman with sharp black eyes.

"I expect girls to arrive on time for this class," she informed the four of them as they took the four unoccupied seats right across the front. "Dawdle in the halls and you'll dawdle in the detention room at four o'clock."

"We weren't dawdling," Suzy said in an indignant voice. "We couldn't find the room. We had to stop and ask, and somebody told us it was upstairs and—"

"That's enough," said Miss Marshall sharply. Anna could see her name printed in big block capitals on the board. "I'm not interested in excuses. The others found the room without any trouble."

Suzy sat and looked injured. Anna was shocked. They hadn't asked anybody the way. She looked over at Maggie. Maggie met her glance and made a face.

Miss Marshall was taking the roll.

"Suzanne Hughes."

"Here," Suzy said, still sounding wounded.

"She's hopeless," Paula muttered under her breath, from Anna's other side. "She fibs all the time, and when you tell her to quit, she doesn't know what you're talking about."

"Paula Kirsch. Is Paula absent?" Miss Marshall's voice reached them.

"Oh, no. I'm here. I'm sorry. I didn't hear—"

"Listen in future," said Miss Marshall, giving Paula a cold look that marked her down as one of the trouble-makers.

Anna, knowing that she, too, was part of this group, felt excited about belonging and uneasy about the day when she would have to explain to the teacher that she, Anna, could not thread a needle. What if Miss Marshall thought she was another Suzy Hughes and just lazy? They were going to do a unit on cooking first. Good. Measuring was the only pitfall there. She was sure already that Maggie would help her when she needed it.

When they moved on to history, Suzy suggested that they sit at the back. Before Anna had time to open her mouth, Maggie said, "No. We're sitting near the front where we can see better."

"You can have lots more fun back there," Suzy protested.

"Go ahead. We'll meet you after," Paula said.

Anna did want them to sit with her, but Suzy made her feel uncomfortable about it. Finally she wrote a note and passed it to Maggie when the teacher had his back turned.

DON'T SIT UP FRONT IF YOU DON'T WANT TO JUST BECAUSE OF ME. I CAN GET ALONG ALL RIGHT.

Maggie passed back the slip of paper.

BUT I DO WANT TO.

Anna felt herself beaming. Suddenly, she thought of Isobel ordering her to smile. She had tried it with Nancy and it hadn't worked. But with Maggie, and Paula too, she didn't even have to think about it. She had done it and so had they. That was the best way with smiles, having them just happen because you couldn't help it. She wrote on the note,

THANKS A LOT.

Maggie read it from where she sat.

"For what?" she asked.

And their grins met like hands clasping.

Nothing special happened in general science, music

appreciation, or art. As they started out once more from the art room, Anna felt tired. Surely noon had come and gone long ago! But she was happy.

I never dreamed I'd be happy, she thought, remembering how she had felt at breakfast.

"Only one more to go," Maggie said, checking the schedule sheet. "P.T."

Physical training! How could somebody be so lighthearted one minute, and then feel nothing but a sense of doom? Isobel had told her the horrors of physical training in full detail.

"I LOVE P.T.," Suzy said.

"How do you know?" Paula asked. "You've never taken it."

"It's sports and dancing and stuff," Suzy said. "I'm great at things like that. I'm going to try out for being a cheerleader. Everybody says they take mostly older girls, but they have to take some from our class. And I've been practicing."

"In front of the mirror?" Paula asked, teasing.

"How did you know?" Suzy looked surprised but not at all embarrassed.

"Just smart, I guess," Paula said.

Isobel had advised Anna to get a doctor's certificate saying she couldn't take part, she remembered now. She fully intended to. She'd go the minute she was free. If only she could survive the next few minutes without making a fool of herself . . .

70

Please, God, don't let there be a relay race, she prayed. There wasn't one.

Miss Willoughby told them that they were to wear tunics, white blouses, navy-blue bloomers, long black stockings, and white running shoes.

Anna was determined to get that doctor's certificate, but she knew she still had to have a tunic for assembly. And it was to be brand-new. Frieda was still wearing Gretchen's old one, so for once Mama had decided that Anna deserved something new. Ever since she had been a little girl she had wanted to wear a school uniform, and now, on assembly days, she really would.

"We have seven minutes left, girls," Miss Willoughby called out, startling Anna out of her daydream. "Spread out quickly in rows, two arms' length apart. Like this."

She pulled two girls forward and demonstrated. The class scrambled into position.

"Now touch your toes. No bending the knees now! Again! Now stretch up high. Up, up, UP! Pretend you're reaching for a star. That's more like it. Arms out. Arms forward. Touch your shoulders. Now let your arms rest at your sides and take a deep, DEEP breath. As much as your lungs will hold! More! Looking around this class, I see some lazy chests! Breathe IN!"

Anna, breathing in, blushed. Her breasts were still small but she was self-conscious about them. The way Miss Willoughby was peering at each of their chests in turn made her want to duck behind someone. Poor Paula!

She was as big as a woman almost. Not that Paula seemed to care.

"Now your posture . . ." Miss Willoughby started.

Mercifully, for Anna, the bell rang. From years of bending over to see things, she had grown slump shouldered. Mama was always at her about standing up straight. While she was used to Mama and hardly heard her anymore, she did not want Miss Willoughby talking pointedly about lazy shoulders.

They headed to their homeroom although Anna did not see how, with Mr. Lloyd in it, it would ever feel like a home. Suzy had dropped back saying something about wanting to find out where you went to ask about getting to be a cheerleader.

"I'll bet she gets to be one too," Paula said, as the three of them walked companionably along together. "She really is pretty and I, having been forced to attend ballet lessons with her for one whole month, can testify that she's graceful. She made the rest of us look like elephants."

"How did you get them to let you quit?" Anna asked, understanding from Paula's tone that ballet lessons had not been her own idea.

"Oh, my mother can see reason if you're firm enough," Paula said. "She thought it would be good for my posture. I told her I'd rather walk around three hours every night with a book on my head."

Anna turned and stared at her. Paula raised her eyebrows.

72

"They're always at me about mine," Anna explained. "I was scared that the P.T. teacher was going to start talking about it. I thought I'd be the only one."

"Oh, I slouch too," Maggie said. "We'll have to form a Poor Posture Club."

Anna was amazed at their nonchalance. Didn't they mind being told, over and over, that they were round-shouldered? To her, it was part of the long list of things she hated about herself.

"There are worse things than poor posture, you know," Maggie said, reading her mind. "The Ten Commandments never say 'Thou shalt not slump.' "

Even Anna had to laugh at that. Maybe she did take things too seriously.

"What do we do now?" Paula wondered. "I'm worn out. I can't even remember the names of all those teachers, and I'm not sure I got that schedule straight. I didn't have time to check it."

"I didn't get it at all," Anna confessed, glad of the opening.

"Come on to the back of the room and you can copy out mine," Maggie said. "While you're doing it, I'll go and sign Paula and me up for locker partners."

Anna, about to copy from Maggie's writing, which was as clear as printing, stopped and looked up anxiously.

"What do I do?" she said. "I don't know anybody."

"I think he'll assign you somebody alphabetically. I'll ask while I'm there," Maggie said. She watched Anna trying to rule off her page into blocks, each space representing a class period.

"Let me do that for you," she offered. "It must be hard to see to get the lines straight."

Anna gladly handed her the ruler.

When she was gone, Anna, looking at the page closely, began to fill in the subjects.

"It's nice getting geography over early in the day," Paula murmured. "If Mr. Lloyd picks on you again, I'll tell my mother."

Anna was puzzled.

"You don't think he shut up just because I talked back to him, do you?" Paula said, her voice low, her expression amused. "My mother's on the Board of Education. And Fred Weber's father is an alderman. We aren't as brave as you think."

"Yes you were brave," Anna said. "He might not even know about your mother . . ."

"He knows," Paula said. "Mother's always getting her picture in the paper. She thinks the strap should be abolished! Anybody who thinks his kid is being treated terribly in school goes to my mother and she makes sure it's checked into. Here's Maggie. What's wrong?"

"I have a lovely surprise for you, Paula," Maggie said, sitting down with a thump on the desk in front of them. "And one for Anna too."

"Don't just sit there looking mad. Tell us," Paula ordered.

"You already had a locker partner," Maggie said to her. "I'll give you three guesses."

"Why that little sneak!" Paula exclaimed. "I never said. . . . She didn't even ask me. . . ."

Anna felt bewildered for an instant; then she guessed the truth.

"Suzy?" she asked.

"Yes indeed. And Mr. Lloyd wasn't about to change anything he considered already settled. That's where Anna's surprise comes in."

Again Paula had it figured out first.

"Smart girl, Maggie," she said. "Wait till I get that Suzy! I'll wring her neck."

"She must have done it that way because she knew you wouldn't agree if she asked," Maggie said slowly. "It's pitiful, in a way. She acts so popular and the boys do like her. Yet we're the only girl friends she has."

"And we don't like her much," Paula said. "Yeah. I can't help feeling kind of sorry for her . . . but she still has her nerve. . . ."

"You don't mind, do you, Anna?" Maggie said. "Because I don't think Mr. Lloyd will let us change either."

Did Maggie mean . . . ? She *must* mean . . .

Anna stopped guessing, afraid she was guessing wrong and would be terribly disappointed.

Paula gave her a friendly nudge.

"Wake up," she said. "She means she's put you down

as her locker partner without asking you. Just another Suzy!"

Anna's face lighted with joy and incredulity.

"I . . . I don't mind," she stammered, so pleased she didn't know what to say. "Don't you . . . mind, that is?"

"If I minded, why would I have done it, dimwit?" Maggie said.

"Here comes Suzy now," Paula said, looking toward the door. "She must be scared but she won't let on. I can hear it already."

Anna bent over her notebook, filling in the last few squares. What on earth would Suzy say and what would Paula do to her? Thank you, Suzy, she thought as she pretended to check over what she had written. Thank you, thank you, thank you.

"Hi there," she heard Suzy say, a little breathless but trying to sound casual. "I found out about where to go to try out for cheerleading. Where were you all? I got back ages ago and you weren't here yet and I . . . Well, people were in line, so . . ."

"I already know, dear partner," Paula said. "Where's our locker?"

Suzy said in a small voice, "Right outside the door. It's number 34. I just thought . . . since we've been friends for so long . . ."

"Ours is really close," Maggie said to Anna. "It's 42."

"Yours?" Suzy said. "You mean, you and Anna . . . ?"

"Sure," Maggie said smoothly. "We had it all planned. Too bad you didn't wait so we could have been right next to each other, eh, Paula?"

"Yeah, too bad," Paula said, her tone mournful. "But we'll keep in touch somehow, Maggie. After all, we've known each other since Grade Four."

Suzy looked uncertainly from one to the other.

"Gee, I'm sorry," she said finally.

"Don't feel you have to apologize, Suzy. It's a mistake anyone might make. Almost anyone," Paula said.

Anna found herself feeling unexpectedly sorry for Suzy, who now looked completely confused. So that was how Paula planned to wring her neck—talk circles around her without ever letting her understand what was happening.

Suzy had been sneaky. But if the others were right, she had done it because she was afraid nobody would want her for a partner.

I got used to it years ago, Anna thought, remembering her brothers and sisters leaving her out of games. And if you can't admit, even to yourself, that you don't have friends, it must be awful pretending and pretending.

"Suzy, thanks a lot," Anna said, surprising herself almost as much as she did the other three.

"What for?" Suzy said.

Anna chose her words carefully.

"For arranging things so I'd have Maggie for my locker partner," she said, "and for . . . for letting me be part of your . . . your . . ."

77

"Gang," Paula said. "With four of us, we surely must be a gang."

Maggie looked at Anna. Paula did too. Anna read, in their eyes, that they were pleased with her and a little ashamed of themselves.

"A gang for sure," Maggie said. "Where'll we meet this afternoon to go book shopping?"

As they settled on a time and place, Suzy was her old, bubbling self.

Then Anna realized, with astonishment, that her first day of high school was over.

And nothing too terrible happened, she thought, dismissing Mr. Lloyd's cruel attack and being lost outside Mr. McNair's room as trifles, now that they were safely past. As a matter of fact, she didn't know when she'd been happier than she was that very minute.

7

ANNA RACED HOME. Yesterday she had thought of confiding today's happenings only to Isobel and, of course, Papa. But Frieda had been sympathetic at breakfast, Mama had waved good-bye to her especially from the door, Gretchen had made beginning possible. They would all be waiting to hear.

But when she burst into the house, only Rudi was there, lounging against the kitchen table, his eyes laughing at her flushed, excited face.

"Oh . . . oh, where are they?" she cried, knowing she was not going to like his answer.

He grinned.

"Papa and Mama at the store; the others not home yet," he said. "But you look as though you have to talk or you'll explode. Why not start with me?"

"You." She looked at him doubtfully.

"Yes, me. I started high school once upon a time myself," Rudi said, his voice still mocking but not mean. "Mind you, I can just barely remember. How was it? Awful? Marvelous? Tell big brother all."

"I have friends!" Anna could not keep the wonder of it bottled up one second longer. "And they all three live just around the corner and up about three blocks on Davenport Road. Maggie and Paula live right next door to each other. And Suzy lives in an apartment across from them. That's how come she latched onto them when she first came."

"Oh," Rudi said, taking this in as though he knew exactly what she was talking about.

Anna plunged into the story of how she had first heard Maggie's voice when Gretchen and she were leaving the office. Then she jumped to losing sight of Nancy French's blouse and then to how Maggie had rescued her and on, all the way to how Suzy had fixed it so that she, Anna, had Maggie for a locker partner. Rudi swung himself up onto the table as she began, and made himself comfortable. Then he listened and listened and listened. Once Anna, in midsentence, stopped and looked at him, certain that he could not really care, but he at once said, "What did she say to *that*?"

"And I'm meeting them to go shopping this afternoon," she finished, "if Mama says it's all right. Maggie gave me her phone number in case it isn't."

"I'm sure it will be fine," Rudi said.

Anna took a deep breath, thought over what she had told him, and realized that there were huge gaps.

"I'm in Mr. Lloyd's homeroom," she said, remembering what Gretchen had told her about Mr. Lloyd and Rudi.

Her brother whistled through his teeth and gave her a sympathetic look.

"That's tough," he said. "He's a nasty man. Doesn't know beans about world history. Just be as quiet as you can and try not to let him notice you."

"That's exactly what Gretchen told me," she said. Rudi was being wonderful. Just the way a big brother should be. He certainly had changed, from the boy who had teased and bullied her when they were younger. He was still looking interested.

"The trouble with that is he's noticed me already," Anna added.

"Mr. Lloyd? How? Because of your eyes?"

"No. Because I'm German," Anna said, her voice slowing as she remembered, and the light dying out of her face. "He picked out the ones he thought had German names. Carl Schmidt and me first. He asked us where our parents came from and then he asked me if I was proud of my Fatherland."

Rudi had straightened up and was staring at her.

"How dared he?" he said. "What did you answer?"

"I was too frightened," Anna said. "And I felt ashamed. But Paula Kirsch—Rudi, she was so brave. She said she was born in Austria right where Adolf Hitler comes from. 'Is this a history lesson?' she asked him."

Rudi's fists clenched. "What did he say to her?"

Anna had known that he would be angry with Mr. Lloyd, but she had not expected the dark rage that had come into her brother's face. She should not have told him. But she would have to finish, now that she had gone this far.

"He just said 'What?' or something. I can't remember exactly. Because right away, another boy said Mr. Lloyd should go on with the roll call and get to him. 'My name's Weber,' he said. Paula told me later that his father's an alderman and her mother is on the Board of Education and that was what gave them the nerve, but I couldn't have said anything if Papa had been Prime Minister!"

Rudi stood up, towering over her, his face twisted with fury.

"He had no right to treat you that way. He should be reported. If only I . . ."

Then he turned away from her and ran from the room. She heard his feet thudding on the stairs and the slam of his bedroom door.

"I should have told him what Mr. McNair said," Anna told the empty room. "The other teachers were all right."

She did not like Miss Marshall and she thought Miss Willoughby was foolish. But they had not been unjust.

She went slowly to the foot of the stairs.

"Rudi," she called. Then, more loudly, "Rudi!"

But her brother did not answer. It was as though she were alone in the house.

It had been a long morning, a morning full of tension, surprise, fear, hurt, joy. Now she suddenly felt exhausted. Rudi's silence behind the closed door, his hopeless anger, weighed on her heart, but she could not think of anything she could do to change what she had done already. Anyway she had to eat lunch. And she had to go to the store and tell Papa and Mama about her morning. She must ask if she could go shopping with the gang.

At that, her smile returned.

She got herself some bread and cheese and poured out a mug of milk. Leaving the empty mug in the sink, she slipped out the front door. The moment the door shut behind her, she felt lighter, as though she had escaped. Partly it was coming out of the darkness inside into the sun-filled noon.

Looking around her, she saw the clouds, fluffy and a dazzling white, racing in the sky. Tree branches waved; leaves rustled. Why, it was breezy! Delighted, she stopped long enough to put on her sweater. Then she began to run.

Soon she slowed to a fast walk. Then she began to sing

softly, but out loud because there was nobody around to
hear her and she wanted to celebrate.

"*I'm going to meet Maggie*
And Paula and Suzy
We're going together
Out shopping for books.

"*Oh, I've got a locker*
And Maggie's my partner
And Suzy is Paula's
And four is a gang!"

A block and a half from the store, she broke into a run
again, hoping no customers would be there when she
arrived.

She opened the door, heard the bell tinkle as she
stepped across the threshold, and stopped dead. Right in
front of her stood her all-powerful older sister Gretchen,
facing Papa and in a flood of tears.

"No, Papa, I don't mean that," she wailed. "I'm not
ashamed of you or Mama. But my real name *is* Margaret.
It is! You know it is."

"And your friends will care more for you if you are
not called Gretchen?" Papa asked, very quietly.

"Not my friends! It's the others. And there's a new
teacher. . . . She said . . . she . . ."

"What did she say, *Liebchen*?" Papa's voice was so
gentle.

84

"Never mind," Gretchen said, giving up and flinging her arms around him. "I've always been Gretchen. I don't know why I thought changing my name would help. Everybody would know anyway. It would probably just make things worse."

A woman came in to buy eggs. Gretchen withdrew into a shadowy corner and mopped her eyes. Anna waited. When another customer came in, so that both Mama's and Papa's attention was taken, she crossed the store to stand beside her older sister.

"I know how it is with the names," she said, her voice just above a whisper. "Mr. Lloyd picked out the German names in the class. I don't want to tell about it. Nothing happened really. He just scared me. I told Rudi and he was so angry, he ran up to his room and slammed the door. When it happened, it made me feel . . . feel . . ."

"Like a criminal," Gretchen finished for her. "Miss Howard told the class that there would be German spies everywhere and warned them to watch out. Then she just looked around at some of us. As if we could be spies! Then, the way she said 'Gretchen.' I thought . . ."

Papa had come up to them without them noticing. From the look on his face, he had heard most of what Gretchen had said.

"Gretchen, running away will not help," he said gently but firmly too. "Were the other teachers like this Miss Howard?"

"No-o," Gretchen admitted, slowly regaining her composure. "A couple of the boys said things . . . but they're mean anyway. The others were the same as always."

"There, then," her father said, smiling at her. "In this case, you must act the adult and leave the teacher to play the child. Isn't that so, Anna?"

Gretchen looked at her younger sister. Anna knew she was waiting for her to tell about Mr. Lloyd. But she also knew Papa, knew him better than anybody in some ways. And she knew that, under his apparent calm, he was so angry at the woman who had hurt Gretchen that it was all he could do to keep his voice level. He was even angrier than Rudi, she thought.

"I made friends, Papa," she told him. She did not have to feign excitement. It seemed more of a miracle every time she thought of it. "They want me to go shopping with them this afternoon. We can get many of our books secondhand at the book exchange from last year's students. May I go, Papa?"

"What are their names?" Mama asked, joining them. "And what do their fathers do?"

Anna sighed. Mama always wanted to know about people's fathers.

"Maggie de Vries and Paula Kirsch," she said, answering the first question. "And Suzy Hughes. I don't know about their fathers, Mama. They didn't say. Paula's mother is on the Board of Education."

Mama pursed up her lips as though she were considering the matter. Anna had an obscure feeling that she would not approve of Paula's mother being on the Board. To Mama's way of thinking, such things were better left to men. Papa laid his hand on top of Anna's head.

"Of course you may go, child," he said. "Have a good time. How much money will she need, Gretchen?"

Gretchen tried to estimate. Mama looked at Anna.

"You haven't eaten and you had nothing for breakfast," she said. "You go nowhere until you eat."

"I had some bread and cheese."

Mama sniffed and began to put together, right there in the store, a lunch big enough to fill someone three times Anna's size: more cheese, a dill pickle, salami, a tomato, bread, cookies, and a McIntosh, one of Anna's favorite kinds of apple.

And while she ate it all, Anna told them about her morning.

In half an hour she was on her way. She was the first one at the meeting place. Then Paula came running down the street.

"Hi, Anna," she called.

Maggie and Suzy arrived two minutes later together.

"Well, here we go," Maggie said as they started for the book exchange.

"Here goes the gang!" Paula sang to "Here Comes the Bride!"

Anna felt like skipping. But acting her age, she marched along with the others.

"Where do we go?" Suzy asked.

Anna was impressed by the casual way in which she put the question. Suzy was the only one of them without older brothers and sisters who had already gone to Davenport Collegiate. Now that she had come safely through the dreaded first morning, Anna was beginning to realize that she knew a lot more about the school than she had thought she did. She had picked up all sorts of bits and pieces of information during the last few years as first Rudi, then Gretchen, and, finally, the twins talked about their days at school. Maggie answered Suzy but Anna could have. She knew all about the secondhand book exchange run by the Student Council.

Suzy stopped walking.

"I have to buy *new* books," she declared. "Mother says secondhand ones have germs."

"What's she afraid you'll catch?" Paula wanted to know.

"I know," Anna said. "Bookworms!"

Maggie and Paula laughed.

"The bookstore people bring in a load of new ones too," Maggie assured Suzy. "But most kids buy as many used books as they can."

"I don't have to get many," Paula said. "Max kept his from last year. The math book is new though, and they studied *Oliver Twist* instead of *Great Expectations*."

"My sister Sarah is so much older than I am that hardly anything is the same," Maggie complained.

"I already have two of the English texts," said Anna. "Papa has all of Shakespeare and Dickens."

"How come?" Suzy asked. "I mean, Nancy French told me your father's a German who runs a grocery store. So why does he have so many books in English?"

"He taught English literature when we lived in Frankfurt," Anna said. For good measure, she added proudly, "He got a degree from Cambridge. Cambridge in England."

"He must be terribly clever," Maggie said, awe in her voice.

Paula was less impressed. "Cambridge in England!" she teased. "I always thought it was in Madagascar."

"He *is* clever," Anna said to Maggie, pointedly ignoring Paula but unable to keep from smiling.

They walked on for a few steps in silence. Then, Suzy, still not satisfied, turned to Anna again.

"If he was a teacher and he's so smart, how come he runs a grocery store now?"

Anna hesitated. It was a long story. How could she make Suzy understand? What did it matter what Suzy thought anyway?

"My Uncle Karl owned the store first," she began. "When he died he left us his grocery store and the house we live in. Right then times were bad in Germany. Papa hated the Nazi party. He was afraid. Everybody was afraid. . . ."

"What was he afraid of? Were the Nazis after him?" Suzy's eyes were gleaming with curiosity.

Anna shook her head, really disliking Suzy for an instant. Papa had not been forced to flee. None of their lives had been endangered. But he had been a hero in a different way. He had decided himself to leave the land he loved in order to raise his children where people were free to speak their thoughts aloud without fear. And he had uprooted the rest of them much against their will. At the time, he had seemed ruthless. Now Anna saw what strength he had shown.

"Suzy Hughes, it's none of your business," Maggie said, sensing Anna's resentment at the prying words. "My father works in a store too, Anna. A shoe store."

"And mine writes for the *Toronto Star*," Paula put in.

"I already know what they do," Suzy said, nettled.

"We're not telling you; we're telling Anna," Paula squelched her. "If her mother's anything like mine, the first thing she'll want to know about us is what our fathers do."

Anna looked down but not quickly enough.

"She's asked you already, hasn't she?" Paula cried.

Anna nodded and Paula laughed.

"Mine already knows about yours," she said. "My dad loves shopping in your store. They talk German together. Tell her my mother's name is Jessie and my father's Gunther. Suzy's father's a lawyer."

"I don't know why it matters to Mama," Anna said. "I don't see what difference it makes."

"She wants your friends to have respectable relations," Maggie said. "Tell her we're so respectable we're boring."

Later Suzy, her arms laden with bright new textbooks, came to find the others. Anna had just located the algebra text and was regarding it with deep misgiving. It was thick, with glossy pages and very small print.

"Don't you like math?" Suzy said, noting her look of dismay.

"I'm not much good at it," Anna murmured.

"Me neither," said Maggie. "Paula can do it herself but can't explain anything to anybody else."

"I'm really good at it," Suzy said, "but it does take a logical mind. I have to go now to meet my mother. We just got home from the cottage on Sunday and I haven't any new school clothes yet. See you tomorrow."

"Think of being an only child with money," Maggie sighed, looking after her.

"And a logical mind," Anna added.

"She's a whiz at math, but if she has a logical mind, I'm a six-toed giraffe," Paula said.

Fifteen minutes later, the three of them staggered out of the school building, their arms full of books.

"I'll never make it home," Maggie gasped.

"I know where we can rest," Paula said. "There's a bench by the bus stop in front of the pet store."

Anna said nothing but she could not have been more delighted. If she had been by herself, she would have stopped there as a matter of course.

The bench was empty. Maggie and Paula unloaded

their books without ceremony, letting them tumble down. Anna took time to place hers in a neat pile. She was not tidy about other things, but Papa had drilled into her from babyhood that a book was a friend and should be treated with respect.

When she joined the other two at the pet-shop window, they were watching three calico kittens having a mock battle in one of the cages while a small gray one slept, curled into a ball, in the corner. Anna looked instead into a cage on the right.

"Hi, Mop," she said softly, reaching up to tap the glass to try to get the puppy's attention.

Maggie and Paula glanced up and followed her gaze.

"Oh, he's darling!" Paula said, crooning the words.

"How do you know his name?" Maggie asked Anna.

"I named him myself," Anna said, looking hard at the puppy as she spoke rather than facing the girls.

"Why?" Maggie said.

Anna was not at all sure they would understand.

"I want a dog," she said slowly, still looking into the cage, "but there's nobody home during the day to look after one. And they cost a lot to feed and all. But last spring I thought, Supposing things change? So I started saving my money just in case. I come by nearly every day and pick out the one I'd like and then I think up a name and come to see him or her. . . . I guess it's pretty dumb really."

"Suppose he gets sold though," Maggie said, smiling

as Mop stood on his hind feet and tried to get at Anna's hand through the glass.

"This is the sixth one I've chosen," Anna said. "I have almost enough to buy one now."

"Does your family know?" Paula inquired.

Anna shook her head.

"They'd feel sorry but they couldn't do anything. But I like choosing one, all the same, knowing that he might be mine if . . ."

Her voice trailed off. She wished she had not explained. It sounded silly, even to her, when she said it out loud. But it hadn't felt that way. Once she had been there when one of her puppies had been sold and she had watched the people taking him away. It had been wonderful because the small boy, who carried him out of the store in his arms, was so clearly holding a dream come true.

"I don't think it's so dumb," Maggie said. "It makes me feel lonesome though. 'Bye, Mop."

They gathered up their books and went on.

"Here's my street," Anna said.

"*Leb' wohl,*" Paula said.

Anna was startled.

"Um . . . *auf Wiedersehen,*" she answered.

"Hey, cut that out," Maggie said. "Or I'll go find a friend who speaks Dutch—not that I know much Dutch."

"I only said 'Farewell,' " Paula translated, "and she said 'Till we meet again,' I guess. Don't worry. I hardly know

93

any German. My father only speaks it when my grandmother is staying with us."

"When we first came, Papa made us practice speaking English every night at supper," Anna said. "I hated it at first. But a year or so ago, he realized that the twins and I were forgetting our German, so now we have to speak German every night instead. He says knowing two languages is like having more than one door into the world."

"Don't let him tell my father that!" Paula said. "Although I don't think my mother would go for it."

"Rule One: No foreign languages to be spoken in this gang," Maggie declared.

"Till Miss Raymond teaches us all French," Anna said.

"That'll be the day!" Paula scoffed. "We'll meet you here, Anna, in the morning about twenty-five to nine, okay?"

Anna tried not to beam but it was hard.

"I'll be here," she promised.

8

DROPPING OFF HER BOOKS at home, Anna went on to the store to call Isobel.

"Hi, Papa . . . Mama," she said, heading for the telephone.

"Anna . . ." Mama spoke a word of warning.

"Good afternoon, Mama," Anna corrected herself, smiling at her mother.

" 'Hello' is all right," Mama pronounced judgment. " 'Hi' is slang. I don't like to hear you children using so much slang. And showing so little respect for your elders."

"Okay," Anna promised, and then saw by the look on Mama's face that she had done it again.

"I'm sorry, Mama. I really am," she said, taking down the receiver and holding it to her ear. She moved closer to the wall so that she could speak into the mouthpiece without being overheard.

"Five minutes, Anna," Papa warned. "This is just the time when people phone in for things they've forgotten and Fritz can still make a few deliveries."

"Number, please," the operator trilled, saving Anna from having to make any promises.

"Walnut 2–0061," Anna said.

"Thank you," replied the disembodied voice, and Anna heard the phone beginning to ring at the Browns.

Before her friend answered, Anna had just time enough to remember that Isobel still had her first day in a strange school ahead of her. So instead of spilling out how exciting and happy her own morning had been, the way she had intended to, she began with, "It's over and I survived!"

"Did my good advice help?" Isobel asked.

"It really did," Anna said, thinking back, "though it wasn't hard, once I met some nice girls. But guess what? My homeroom teacher is Mr. Lloyd!!"

"Oh, NO." Isobel groaned. "I escaped him last year but I heard enough about him to fill a book!"

Anna ran through her whole list of teachers before Papa told her to hang up. He was especially lenient. They had talked for fully fifteen minutes. Maybe twenty.

In spite of Isobel's interest in everything, it seemed to

96

Anna that she was worried about her own new school. Anna wished she could help somehow. But just as Isobel had not been able to go to school in her place, she would not be able to face Isobel's first day for her. Some things you had to do by yourself.

She found herself humming a song Mrs. Schumacher had taught them. She had liked it although it was sad, but, until now, she had not really felt it meant anything. She sat down on the chair Papa had placed behind the counter for Mama. Mama never took time to sit on it but Papa insisted on leaving it there, in case. As Anna waited for her parents to close the store so she could walk home with them, she sang the song softly, barely loud enough for herself to hear.

> *"I've got to walk that lonesome valley.*
> *I've got to walk it by myself.*
> *There's nobody else can walk it for me.*
> *I've got to walk it by myself."*

Yet it hadn't been lonesome because of Maggie. The others too, but Maggie especially.

She thought about the four of them, trying to figure out what each one was like.

Paula's the leader, she thought. She's brave and she decides things. Suzy's the . . . the popular one.

She stopped, searching for a better word to describe Suzy, because the others had said Suzy wasn't well liked by most of the girls.

"Although the boys think she's the icing on the cake," Paula had declared.

So maybe "popular" was all right. She certainly was the prettiest of the four of them.

And I'm the homeliest, Anna thought ruefully. Maybe if Paula's the leader, I'm the follower. I'm the person who's under their wing.

She was pretty sure that they weren't letting her go around with them simply because they felt sorry for her, although she did know that was part of it. But she didn't know yet what she had to give to them, how she would find her place and fit in. Maybe I have some hidden talent, she told herself. I hope, I hope.

That left Maggie.

That's easy, Anna thought. She's the kind one. Already she felt Maggie and she were real friends. She touched the wooden counter to be safe.

On the way home, she told Mama what the other three girls' fathers did for a living.

"They sound like fine people," Mama said after a thoughtful pause. "It is good that you befriend their daughters."

Anna gasped. Didn't Mama realize that she, Anna, was the one who was being befriended? Papa put a hand on her shoulder and squeezed it gently.

When supper was ready, she went to call the boys. Fritz was in the backyard practicing throwing baskets through an improvised hoop he and Rudi had put up on a tree. Rudi was up in his room with the door closed.

"Time to eat," Anna called in to him.

He didn't answer. Thinking he might be asleep, she banged loudly on his door.

Her brother jerked the door open and scowled at her.

"I heard you the first time," he said. "I'm not Superman, you know—faster than a speeding locomotive, more powerful than . . ."

"It's 'faster than a speeding bullet, more powerful than a locomotive,' " Anna corrected him.

"He can leap tall buildings at a single bound!" shouted Rudi, and jumped all the way down to the landing.

Still laughing, Anna followed him in to the table.

Before Papa could ask the blessing, though, Rudi, who had been acting so silly with her only seconds before, spoke in a voice tight with strain.

"I do not wish to speak German tonight, Papa."

There was a startled silence.

Then Ernst Solden turned to his son.

"Rudi, I think I know what you are feeling," he said in his usual quiet voice, "but German is our first language, the language of Goethe and—"

"And Hitler! Papa, have you read today's paper?" Rudi cried. "Have you listened to the news? Do you know what is happening in Poland? Papa, don't you care?"

"My son," Papa started, his voice still quiet but heavy now.

Then Mama broke in. "I have read. I have listened,"

Klara Solden said. "My mother's mother was Polish. We went to Warsaw in the summers to visit. We children stayed up late playing in the garden. . . ."

Nobody knew what to say. Even Rudi looked down, away from the pain in his mother's usually soft, cheerful face.

"Ernst, we will speak English," she said to her husband.

Without further protest, Papa bowed his head and asked the blessing in English. When he had finished, nobody spoke or began to eat for a long moment. Then Fritz reached for a roll.

"I forgot the butter," Mama said, and fled to the kitchen.

"The butter's here!" Gretchen called after her. They could all hear Mama crying.

"You prayed for the hurt people, Papa, but you forgot to say thank you for the food," Frieda said, her mind focusing on the one thing that seemed safe to mention.

"I couldn't speak of the food on our table when so many have no homes," Papa said. "But this is not the time to dwell on that. Pass your plate, Anna, for some goulash or whatever this is that Gretchen has concocted. We must do our best to go on living fully, joyously even. We mustn't forget to laugh."

Mama, empty-handed and self-conscious, returned to the table. Rudi, his eyes shocked, stared at his father.

"Laugh!" he said. "How can we laugh?"

"I don't know how but we must," Ernst Solden said,

passing Anna's plate back and accepting Gretchen's. "Because the world is going insane, should we go mad? That is no solution. Laughter, good, honest laughter, is one of the sure signs of sanity."

"I've seen lots of pictures of Hitler smiling," Gretchen said slowly, "but I don't think I've ever seen one of him laughing."

"No," her father said. " 'He smiles and smiles and is a villain.' "

Mama surprised them by laughing at that.

"Ernst, if you were on your deathbed," she said, a little hysterically, "I believe you would find something to quote. I remember those lines. Is it *Othello* or *Hamlet*?"

Papa beamed at her as though she were one of his more backward pupils who had just stunned everyone by coming up with the right answer. "*Hamlet*. Act One. Scene—"

"Stop!" Fritz said. "If there's one thing I can't stand, it's Shakespeare. We had to do *As You Like It* last year and, boy, was it dull! Hardly any of it made sense and it was so old-fashioned. He didn't say anything that meant anything."

"That a son of mine should speak that way of Shakespeare," Papa said, looking sorrowfully at Fritz.

Fritz grinned at him good-naturedly.

"That a father of mine can't fix a leaking tap!" he said.

Anna was on Papa's side. She could not understand Fritz's dislike of all that had to do with reading. Papa

101

had been choosing things for her to memorize ever since she could remember. It was one of her best gifts from him, a headful of poems. He made her remember the author's name always, so she already knew several bits of Shakespeare's writing even though she had yet to study one of his plays in school. Papa had chosen a new piece for her to learn just last week, and suddenly, she saw why.

"If you only knew, Fritz," she said. "Shakespeare said something that isn't one bit old-fashioned. Not much anyway. It talks about right now. About soldiers in wartime."

"I'll bet," Fritz scoffed.

"Papa, you tell him," Anna begged.

"Have you forgotten it so soon?" her father teased, knowing she hardly ever forgot, that she could still recite things he had taught her when she was four and five. "You start and I'll help if you get stuck."

Everyone was watching her. She cleared her throat and took a deep breath to steady herself. She wanted to do the words justice.

"Once more unto the breach, dear friends, once more,
Or close the wall up with our English dead.
In peace, there's nothing so becomes a man
As modest stillness, real humility,
But when the blast of war blows in our ears,
Then imitate the action of the tiger.
Stiffen the sinews, summon up the blood . . .

"Then there's a part I didn't learn and then . . . how does it start, Papa?"

" 'For there is none of you . . .' " her father prompted.

" '. . . none of you so base and mean,' " Anna picked it up:

> "*That hath not noble lustre in your eyes.*
> *I see you stand like greyhounds in the slips,*
> *Straining upon the start. The game's afoot.*
> *Follow your spirits, and upon this charge,*
> *Cry, 'God for Harry, England and Saint George!' "*

"You're pretty smart, Anna," Fritz said with genuine admiration. "I don't see how you can learn stuff like that. It sounds warlike, all right. Who's Harry?"

"Henry the Fifth," Papa answered for her. The English were badly outnumbered and all the odds were against them, but they followed his lead and won."

As he went on explaining, turning supper into a history lesson, Mama said, slipping into German, "Gretchen, pass the salt, please."

Anna noticed the switch to the other language but nobody else seemed to. Nobody else seemed to notice Rudi either, but perhaps she did only because she was sitting right next to him. He was staring down at his right hand, clenched into a hard fist, on the table edge.

" 'Follow your spirits . . .' " he said in a whisper.

Anna, recognizing the words as part of the speech she

had just recited, opened her mouth to finish out the line for him.

"But how can I?" he asked, still talking to himself. Just in time, Anna knew that he had not meant anyone to hear and she remained silent. Another phrase from the famous lines jumped into her mind.

" 'Straining upon the start . . .' "

That was how Rudi looked. But he could not be thinking of going to war! You had to be a man, and Rudi was still a boy.

"Anna, your papa has asked you for the butter twice," Mama said, reproof in her voice.

Anna passed it. When she turned again to look at her big brother, he had his head bent and was eating quickly, as though he were ravenous.

She had been all wrong. Whatever he had meant, she had obviously misunderstood. Perhaps she had not even heard him correctly. He had spoken very softly.

She picked up her own fork and began to eat.

Then the song that had been haunting her ever since she talked with Isobel came floating back.

> *"He must go and stand his trial.*
> *He has to go there by himself.*
> *There's nobody else can go there for him.*
> *He has to stand it by himself."*

Where is the lonesome valley? she thought.
And she was afraid.

9

ANNA'S FIRST P.T. CLASS was scheduled for Friday afternoon. On Thursday after school, she went to see Dr. Schumacher. His waiting room was so crowded that she had to stand for twenty minutes before there was a chair free. On a table were battered old copies of *The Saturday Evening Post*, *Chatelaine*, *Life*, *Parents'*, *MacLeans*, and *The Ladies' Home Journal*, but Anna instead opened the book she had brought with her. She always brought a book because she could not bear reading half a story and never learning how it ended. Maggie had loaned her the novel she was about to begin. It was *A Girl of the Limberlost* by Gene Stratton Porter.

105

From the moment she read the first chapter heading, Anna's sympathies were with the heroine, Elnora Comstock.

WHEREIN ELNORA GOES TO HIGH SCHOOL AND LEARNS MANY LESSONS NOT FOUND IN HER BOOKS.

She soon discovered that Elnora's troubles were much worse than her own had been. Mrs. Comstock sounded hateful, the meanest mother Anna had met in a book. Elnora's clothes were all wrong. So was her lunchbox. She had not the money she needed to buy books and pay her tuition, and she didn't know anybody. No Gretchen helped her and no Maggie befriended her later. There seemed to be only one thing in her favor and that was her ability at math. Anna sighed but hurried on down the page.

Then, without warning, a hand took hold of the book and pulled it down away from Anna's face. Anna jumped and gasped. She had been so lost in the world inside the story that she had completely forgotten where she really was. The woman who still grasped the corner of *A Girl of the Limberlost* was a total stranger. Anna stared at her in bewilderment.

"You don't know me, dearie, so don't look so taken aback," announced this stranger. "Pearl Whittaker's my name, Mrs. Robert J. I'm sure your mother's told you not to talk to strangers and she's quite right. But I just had to speak to you to keep you from ruining your eyesight!"

Anna felt herself flushing.

How does she know about my eyes? she thought. Mama did *not* tell me not to talk to strangers.

"If you hold your book up that close, you'll strain your eyes terribly, dear, and you'll get headaches, if you don't go blind. Hold it at least fourteen inches away. There. That's about right. Look and you'll see for yourself how much better it is."

Anna stared down at the page. She could not distinguish a single word. Pulling her scattered wits together, she did her best to speak up for herself, meanwhile trying to ignore the fact that everyone in the room was staring at her.

"I can't see that far away . . ." she began, angry at herself because her voice, which she tried to make firm, sounded thin and wavery. Mrs. Whittaker did not let her finish.

"Of course you can, if you try. You've just got into bad reading habits. You've let your eyes grow lazy! Unless your glasses are too weak. I must say they look thick enough but I'll tell Dr. Schumacher you need them checked," she said, finally letting go of the book and settling herself more comfortably on her chair.

Anna, cringing with mortification, ordered herself to lift the book up to where she could see and get back to Elnora but her hands refused to obey. Maybe it was because they were shaking so. She shoved them hard against her knees to still them. Then she concentrated on looking at nothing and nobody.

When her blush had faded and she was even beginning

107

to see that there might be a funny side to all of this, once she got in to talk to Dr. Schumacher, she heard Mrs. Whittaker talking in what was supposed to be a low voice to another lady.

". . . so she phoned yesterday and asked to have her records sent to Dr. Thornfield. I said to her, 'I know what you mean, Agnes, but even if he is German, he's been my doctor for thirteen years and he brought Herbie into the world after I'd given up hope of ever having a boy.' "

The other woman laughed at that.

"He's been here since he was a young man," she said. "He's Canadian now, I say. He doesn't even have an accent and he's married one of our girls. I do wonder though if he'd be able to join up. . . . Blood's thicker than water, if you know what I mean."

"Well, somebody has to go," a third woman said, her voice not quite low enough for Anna to miss. "And Doctor hasn't any children. Jim wanted to enlist, if you can imagine. I told him he'd just better not try it, leaving me to cope with his three boys!"

"Mrs. Whittaker, the doctor will see you now," Miss Willis said.

Good riddance, thought Anna. She grabbed up her book, defying anyone else to challenge her.

Until the receptionist got to her, she was able to push aside what she had heard the women saying and return to Elnora. Dr. Schumacher left her till last so she had just finished Chapter Four when her turn finally came.

Things were looking decidedly brighter for Elnora so it was not too hard to close the book till later.

"I understand you need much stronger lenses in your glasses," Franz Schumacher said, holding the door open for her.

He was smiling as he spoke. Letting go of her anger and embarrassment, Anna smiled too.

"Did you know that she is not going to go to another doctor, even though you are German, because you brought Herbie into the world after she had given up hope?" she told him, taking the chair opposite his desk.

"Poor Herbie," Dr. Schumacher said. "I'm not sure I did him any favor. Pearl means well, but she has not one ounce of perception. You must have got quite an earful out there, if they got onto us Germans."

Anna, who had been thinking about herself and her book, now ran over in her mind the conversation she had overheard. She had joked about it but, suddenly, she saw nothing funny in it after all. She sat very still, staring at Franz Schumacher, who had met the Soldens at the train station the night they first arrived in Toronto and who was her oldest friend in some ways. Had Agnes, whoever she was, really changed doctors because this man had been born in Berlin? What had all the rest meant? "Blood is thicker than water, if you know what I mean," for instance.

One of them had said Dr. Schumacher didn't have an

accent. Anna had understood that that was a point in his favor.

But Mama had an accent. Even Papa did, though his was less noticeable.

"Anna, don't look so worried," Dr. Schumacher said gently. "What does it matter what one silly woman says?"

"There were three of them," Anna said, her voice low.

"Three then. Did they think I should enlist?"

Anna thought about it.

"They thought you should but I think they didn't want you to because you're their doctor," she said. "Oh, I don't know. I was only half listening. I wanted to get on with my book."

He laughed and asked her why she had come. She explained about needing a certificate to help her escape P.T. He shook his head at that, telling her she needed to be physically fit.

"I wouldn't mind that part," Anna said, "but you don't understand what it's like to be in a class like that when you can't see properly. Isobel told me about it but it's already happened to me enough other times, trying to play games and things, for me to know what she means. They run relay races, and every time a runner comes back she passes you a stick. When you can't see, you mostly drop it and have trouble picking it up and then don't run straight to the right place and you lose the race for your entire team."

"They must do other things though," he said.

"Yes. They teach you the schottische and folk dances and the teacher always says things like, 'First you do this and then move this arm that way.' And everybody else can see what she's doing so you're the only one who has no idea what she's talking about. They play basketball and volleyball and baseball and dodgeball, and I can't catch any ball, especially when I'm not expecting it or when it's as small as a softball. I can catch grounders because I can hear them coming, but you don't use grounders in a basketball game. Exercises are like the folk dancing. I can't think of anything good about any of it."

"Too bad they don't have a swimming pool at that school," he said. "I'm certain there must be something good, Anna, but I admit that it sounds like a nightmare."

He rummaged in his desk for paper.

"I'll give you a letter to this Miss Willoughby telling her to let you yourself be the judge of what you can do. That means you have to play fair and do anything you can."

"I will. I promise," Anna said.

He handed her the envelope but, as she got up to go, he stopped her.

"I left you till last on purpose," he said. "Eileen phoned about something and I told her you were here. She wants me to bring you home to supper so we can hear all about school. We have something special to tell you too. Your father said you may come, so it's all arranged. What do you say?"

Anna was delighted.

"Let's go," she said.

They got into Franz Schumacher's old Ford car. It had started to rain, so he drove slowly.

"How's your father?" he asked Anna. "I'm sure the war's come as a shock to him."

"I guess so," Anna murmured. She had not confided in anyone the grief she had seen on her father's face last Sunday morning. By the time the others had assembled, he had regained his self-control. Anna felt it had been too private a thing to share, even with Dr. Schumacher now, although he was her father's closest friend in Canada. Her answer did seem inadequate so she added, "He never misses a news broadcast."

"What do you think about it yourself?"

She had not expected the question and had no idea how to answer.

"It just doesn't seem . . . real," she said finally, embarrassed that she could not think of anything significant to say. Adults so seldom asked for your opinion on a serious matter. "Germany is so far away to me now," she added. "Wars in books seem full of danger and excitement and brave deeds. But so far, nothing has been anything like that. It would be different if I lived in Poland."

"That is very true," he said dryly. "But don't feel ashamed, Anna. Many of us share your feelings. I cannot take it in either. It is unreal to me also, since I came to Canada when I was about Rudi's age. That won't be true

112

for your parents though. They must have many friends and even relatives still in Germany."

"Not so many," Anna said. "Friends, yes. But the only near relative is my Aunt Tania. She's Papa's younger sister."

"I've heard him speak of her. She's married, isn't she?"

"Not now," Anna said. "Uncle Tobias died of a heart attack about three years ago."

"Have you had word from her recently?"

"Not since last spring and then it was just a note to say she was well and had work doing translations for a businessman and for us not to worry."

"In that case, we had better speak of something else," Dr. Schumacher said. "We can't help her with our talk. Has Rudi started school yet?"

"In a few days," Anna answered, glad to leave the topic of Aunt Tania behind. Not that she did not care about her, not that she did not remember her with love, but she felt guilty because most of the time, Aunt Tania was faraway and unreal too. It was wrong of her to think only of herself and school and the gang, but she couldn't help it.

"For Rudi, it must seem more real," the man beside her said, as though he had followed her thoughts. "Rudi must wonder what the boys he knew are doing."

Anna had not considered that. If she were to move away from Toronto tomorrow, she would certainly remember it very clearly, especially the people. Isobel, the

Schumachers themselves, Maggie, Miss Sutcliff . . . Was that why Rudi dreamed about Wolf and the other boy whose name she had now forgotten? Helmut, that was it.

Dr. Schumacher parked the car and they got out and ran for the house. Before they reached the door, however, he caught her by the arm and said in a quiet but urgent voice, "Anna, don't talk about the things we have been discussing tonight, will you? Eileen has enough on her mind. She wants to hear about school."

"There's a lot I want to tell her," Anna said, glad not to have to discuss the worrying things.

"Be especially kind to your Papa though," Dr. Schumacher said. "Not that you are ever anything else, I know."

Then Mrs. Schumacher was taking Anna's wet coat and draping it over a chair next to the fireplace.

"I thought we'd eat in here," she said, "and have a fire since it's so chilly. Tonight it's hard to believe Tuesday was so warm and bright. Just let me bring in our plates and you can start at the beginning and tell me the whole thing. I can see already that it wasn't nearly as bad as you thought it was going to be."

Anna knew she shouldn't talk with food in her mouth but several times, she couldn't help it. She had so much to tell and they listened with such genuine interest and enjoyment. She finally came to the end just as it was time to bring in the dessert. It was only then that she remembered Dr. Schumacher had said they had some news to tell her as well. She began to apologize, ashamed of herself.

"Anna, don't apologize. We wanted to hear about you first. We've been in suspense all week. I did talk to your mother on the phone but she couldn't tell me all the details the way you have," Mrs. Schumacher said, putting her hand on Anna's. "Now, as for what we have to tell you, it shouldn't be such a big surprise after three years. We're expecting a baby. Sometime in April, we think."

Anna put down her pie fork and stared from one to the other, her face ablaze with delight.

"A baby!" she said, as though they were the first people ever to have thought of such a thing.

"I knew you'd be pleased," her old teacher said, with a laugh that shared in Anna's joy. "You're the fourth person we've told. You may tell your family but we're not going to make it known generally yet. I'll have to let the school authorities know as I'll be stopping teaching at Christmas. But it's a bit early to start all the tongues wagging."

Anna suddenly thought of something.

"Now they won't be able to say you haven't children," she blurted, without thinking.

Seeing their startled expressions, she longed to take the words back somehow. Since that was impossible, she had to explain.

"Those women . . . when they were talking about you . . . enlisting . . . they said . . ." she stumbled.

"What women?" Mrs. Schumacher demanded.

"Oh, just some gossips in my waiting room," Dr. Schumacher explained. "I suppose they said I shouldn't hesitate to join up because, after all, I have no offspring, eh, Anna?"

She nodded unhappily.

"You're right," he said. "They won't be able to say that soon. They may say though that we're having this baby for that very reason."

"Franz, how can they!" his wife cried. "Why don't you tell them the truth about yourself?"

It was Anna's turn not to comprehend.

"He tried to join the army yesterday," Mrs. Schumacher said, "even though we were sure about the baby by then. He thought they'd take him, because they'd need doctors, in spite of a heart murmur he has as result of having rheumatic fever years ago. It's nothing to worry about but they wouldn't accept him, thank goodness."

"They may yet, before it's all over," her husband said in a low voice.

"Oh," Anna said. "Of course, when they find out about that, they won't be able to say anything. Maybe even that Agnes person will come back."

"What Agnes person?" Mrs. Schumacher said. Even her husband looked blank, for a moment. Then he looked at Anna, with dawning comprehension.

"A lady who has taken herself, her dizzy spells, her bunions, and her obesity to Dr. Thornfield. Long may she remain with him, poor man. I heard she'd called. I

116

should have guessed Pearl would know all about it, too, since she and Agnes have adjoining back fences." He laughed as he spoke, but there was not much mirth in his laughter.

He stood up suddenly and began prowling about the room as though he were too restless to stay in one place.

"You two don't understand a couple of things, however," he went on, glancing at them and then away. "First, I can't tell my patients about my heart condition because my pride will not allow me to. Second, even if I did tell them, those who are ready to turn against me would not believe a word I said. A heart murmur isn't obvious, you know. If I had only one leg, now, that would help. If I was wearing a hearing aid, on the other hand, it might be argued that I didn't really need it, especially if I had acquired it within the last year or so."

"Franz, stop. It's not like you to be so cynical because of one silly woman whom you don't even like," Eileen Schumacher said. "Come back and sit down. Anna hasn't started on her pie and you've left half of yours. When I make pie, I expect it to be eaten with relish."

Anna laughed.

"For the longest time, I thought that meant pickle relish," she said. "The kind you put on hot dogs."

"The English language is full of words with double meanings like that," her old teacher answered, immediately taking the bait as Anna had known she would. When Mrs. Schumacher had been Miss Williams, her class had learned several sure ways of distracting her. One was a discussion of the peculiarities to be found in English.

Dr. Schumacher, sitting down again, smiled. As their glances met, Anna realized that he too had discovered this way of changing the subject.

"Have you any good names to suggest for this baby?" he asked. "We don't promise to use what you suggest, but we are beginning to collect and consider names."

"When I have my children," Anna said dreamily, "I'm going to name the boys Sebastian, Timothy, and Matthew and the girls Melissa, Jocelyn, and Charlotte."

"You're planning on six, three of each?" Dr. Schumacher looked amused.

"Just because you have the names ready doesn't mean you have to use them," Anna defended herself, returning to her pie. "I change my mind all the time. I read a book today about a girl called Elnora. I never met anyone called that."

"A Girl of the Limberlost!" Mrs. Schumacher said, looking pleased with herself. "I loved that book."

The time of tension passed. From then until Dr. Schumacher drove her home, Anna enjoyed every minute.

He came in with her for a few moments. "I guess you want to tell them yourself," Anna said, reaching out to open the door.

"No. You go ahead," he said.

"I'll start knitting a shawl tomorrow," Mama cried when Anna had broken the news. Anna stayed and listened to the congratulations.

"Now you'll really find out what trouble is," Papa teased his friend, "especially if it's a girl."

Anna protested with the rest and then, the first moment she could get away, escaped to sit on her bed and get back to Elnora Comstock's story. It was after eleven when she finished it, and she realized she had not done any homework at all.

10

THE SOLIDARITY OF THE GANG began to give in the middle of the second week of school when Suzy, to nobody's surprise, did become a cheerleader. Practice now claimed her promptly at four, so she could no longer walk home with the others. She was so pleased about it though that they could not help but rejoice with her and even take pride in having her as their friend. Suzy was not noted for either her tact or her insight, but when she was happy she was radiant.

A couple of days later Paula had an announcement to make too.

"I've decided to join the Dramatic Society."

They plied her with questions and learned she had a

secret longing to try being an actress and, the night before, she had made up her mind to stop being secretive about it and find out if she really had any ability. "They put on three plays a year," she said, "so if I'm good at all, I should get a part in one of them."

"So you'll be busy at four too," Maggie said. "My great news is that, starting tomorrow, I'm going to be bringing my lunch and eating at school."

"How come?" Paula asked. "I thought your mother agreed with mine that the walk did us good."

"She does, but she's not going to be home at noon for a while because she's got a job looking after an old lady with a broken leg who won't go to the hospital because she's sure they'd kill her off there somehow. Mum's a trained nurse, you know. I hate having to be the only one taking my lunch."

"You won't be," Anna said, delighted at this turn of affairs. "Mama can't come home at noon because the store is busy then, so I eat that kind of lunch anyway. We make everybody's the night before. I would have taken it to school long ago, the way the twins and Gretchen are doing, but I hadn't anyone to eat with."

As she spoke, she thought, I'm glad it's Maggie I'll be with.

It was Paula who said slowly, "The gang won't be meeting so much then. Of course, every so often, we may all meet in the detention room."

They laughed at that, but nobody liked the thought of being apart so much even though they had been a foursome for only a couple of weeks. Then a milk wagon came around the corner and their downhearted mood was gone as they waited for Paula to feed the horse.

"Hi-yo, Silver!" Paula said, seeing the horse was mostly white.

She dug into her pocket and came up with four sugar cubes. Paula always carried them for the next time she would meet a horse. Her longing for a horse of her own was like Anna's hope for a puppy. They both still made up daydreams in which somehow it all came true and there they were with their faithful animals. It was nice there were lots of horse-drawn delivery wagons and the pet store right on the way to and from school.

The horse clopped off. Anna remembered that she had brought a poem she had discovered the night before. She told them about it as she looked for the place in her book.

"It's by Emily Dickinson too," she said.

There was no need to say more. Miss Sutcliff had told them she thought maybe Emily Dickinson was her favorite poet. Miss Sutcliff was everybody's favorite teacher—everybody's but Suzy's, who got fluttery whenever Mr. McNair asked her to go to the board.

"It's the way he calls me 'Suzy,' " she said, with a long sigh.

Anna was just thankful that so far Mr. McNair had not asked her to do a math problem at the board. As she never raised her hand to give an answer either, she had only heard him call her "Anna" a couple of times when he had asked about Rudi. It was a nice change. Most of the teachers called the boys simply by their surnames and the girls Miss Hughes or Miss Solden. It was flattering in a way, but distant.

"Here's the poem," she said, standing still to get a better hold on her other books so she could lift the poem up to read it.

"Anna, we're going to be late if we don't keep moving," Paula said.

They all knew what that meant. Mr. Lloyd never accepted an excuse, no matter how valid. You were sent to the principal's office for a late slip and given a detention when you had three of them. They had been given one only two days before, when Suzy's mother offered to drive them and then dawdled about it just long enough to make them arrive one minute after the bell.

"I can read and walk at the same time," Anna said. "You'll like this. It's funny. It makes me feel as if I actually knew her. Listen."

Holding the book so close that it nearly touched her nose, she began to read aloud.

> *"I'm nobody. Who are you?*
> *Are you nobody too?*
> *Then there's a pair of us. Don't tell.*
> *They'd banish us, you know.*
> *"How dreary to be somebody;*
> *How public, like a frog*

To tell your name the livelong day
To an admiring bog!"

Paula laughed. Anna turned her head to share in her appreciation of the fun in the rhyme. As she did, she tripped over the curb and would have gone flying if Maggie had not had quick enough reflexes to grab her.

"Anna Solden, watch where you're going!" she scolded.

"Thanks. I will from now on, truly. But don't you like that poem? I wonder if she wrote it to somebody real. I'd love to have somebody write a poem like that to me," said Anna.

"I'll do one to you. It's easy," Paula said. "Give me two seconds to get feeling poetic."

Forgetting the danger of being late, she stood stock-still, put her right hand over her heart, and regarded Anna solemnly.

> *"I'm somebody. That I know.*
> *Heaven knows who you are though.*
> *I think I know you but right in the middle,*
> *You come out wrong and turn into a riddle.*
> *A frog in a bog has better eyes*
> *Than you, you say. Then, to my surprise,*
> *You see just fine. Still, since you're my friend,*
> *That makes you somebody too.*
>   *The End."*

Anna stared at her in awe. The other two laughed.

"She can rhyme them off as easy as a wink," Suzy bragged as though she had invented Paula. "You should hear the *awful* one she made up about me last year. It was a scream. How does it go, Paula? I just hated it."

"You loved it, you mean," Maggie said. "It's a wonder you didn't have it tattooed on your forehead."

"Jealousy will get you nowhere," Suzy countered without turning a hair.

Paula, now walking along and looking much as usual, grinned at Anna.

"I learned to do it from my father," she said. "He does it all the time. We don't make up our own poems, just parodies of other people's. I'm no good at writing the kind of poem you think up all by yourself. I did Suzy's to 'The Charge of the Light Brigade.'"

Immediately Suzy began chanting:

> *"Boys to the left of her,*
> *Boys to the right of her."*

"Quit it," Paula ordered. "I did really like what you read, Anna. I know what you mean about feeling like you know her. She sounds as though she was shy."

"I think she was," Anna said absently. Right now she wanted to learn why Paula had said in her bit of rhyme:

> *You . . . turn into a riddle.*

Maybe Paula had said it on purpose to get her to ask.

"What did you mean . . . about me being a riddle?" she asked, looking at the squares of sidewalk she was walking over instead of at Paula. She took care not to step on a crack while she waited to hear.

Paula's hesitation lasted only a moment, however, for she was a forthright person and Anna had guessed rightly that she did want to discuss this very puzzle.

"It's not just me. We all feel muddled. We talked about it that day you went to the doctor's and didn't wait for us. We know you don't see well. You told us so yourself and, anyway, it's pretty obvious. Yet, every so often, you seem to see perfectly."

"Half the time, I forget about you not being able to see," Maggie confided. "You just seem like anybody. And then, I realize you hardly ever can see what's on the board even when you're up front, while I can see that from the very back of the room."

Anna had taken her limited vision for granted for so long now that their bewilderment caught her off guard. While she tried to think of what to say, Paula plunged on.

"Yesterday when you came to meet us, I could tell you knew where I was even though I was standing right beside a bunch of people waiting for the bus—and I was way farther away from you than any blackboard."

"You had on your red plaid skirt," Anna said, "and your yellow sweater. I wouldn't have known you except that I recognized the color of your clothes. I didn't see your face or anything. Sometimes I've thought I recognized people and I've waved, and then when I got close I found out I'd made a mistake. Now I just smile until I know I'm right."

She was figuring out the answer as she went along. As she came to a halt, she realized that she knew something new about herself. She had sensed it but had never before defined it in words.

They were close to the school now. She suddenly had a lot more to say. She tried to put it all into a few quick sentences but it was too complicated.

"I'm like you, Maggie. I don't think about not seeing till I'm up against something I can't see. At home, where I know where everything is, I run and never think of falling. But as soon as I'm in a strange place, I have to watch out for steps and stuff."

"You look around just like the rest of us," Paula commented. "You don't seem to be missing anything."

"To me, what I see seems normal," Anna answered. She smiled, perceiving it as funny rather than sad. "I don't see what I'm missing, so I don't think I'm missing anything. Mostly, I just feel ordinary. Until I need help," she finished, a bit abashed at so much talk about herself.

"I just don't understand what you DO see," Maggie said in frustration.

"I don't either, exactly," said Anna. "I asked Dr. Schumacher that and he made it a bit easier for me to understand. He said that I can see at twenty feet what you see at about one hundred. If we are both standing looking at a door, for instance, I see the door and you see the door—but you also maybe see the doorknob and the keyhole and the grain of the wood. I just know there's a door there. I see as far as you do, more or less, because we can both see to the horizon, but everything's dimmer and less distinct for me."

Suzy had been silent throughout this whole discussion. Now she put a hand out and clutched Anna by the elbow, jolting her so that she almost missed her step.

"I think it's awful asking you things like that," she said. "It's bad enough to . . . to be different and not to see . . . but it isn't kind to talk about it. I don't see how you can be so unfeeling as to . . . to discuss it as though it were any other fact," she said to Maggie and Paula. "It's cruel!"

Anna, for the first time since Paula had made up the rhyme which had started off the whole conversation, felt embarrassed. Not only embarrassed but furious. Suzy made her poor eyesight sound like a shameful secret, something to be hidden away and talked about only in whispers when the afflicted person was out of earshot. She jerked her arm free and tried to think of something to say that would finish Suzy's gushing over her.

"Oh, shut up," Maggie said, "and get that drippy look off your face, Suzy Hughes. Anna doesn't have two heads or . . . or . . ."

"Her foot in her mouth," Paula said. "Which is where yours is. How can we help her if we don't know when she needs help? Who would know better than Anna herself?"

"The trouble is," Anna said, as they hurried up the steps and down the hall to their lockers, "that sometimes I don't know when I need help because I don't see what I'm not seeing so I don't know I'm not seeing it."

Suzy refused to laugh but the other two made up for it.

"We'll just have to keep on playing it by ear," Maggie said. "But you'll understand that if we make mistakes, it's only because you have us thoroughly confused."

They reached their desks in the nick of time. Anna, catching her breath, thought of Mrs. Schumacher. Hadn't she said something about Anna not really knowing herself what she could do and what she couldn't, when and how to ask for help, and when to manage on her own? She should have known that her old teacher would be right.

I wonder if I'll ever really know though, she thought. If I were really blind, it would be simple compared to this.

She looked across the aisle at Maggie. Maggie was getting out the map of the Great Lakes they had had to draw. Anna had an enlarged copy that Maggie had made for her especially. She started to turn to her own book when the sun came from behind a cloud and turned Maggie's wheat-brown hair into a bright halo.

129

Anna knew right then that while it might be simpler to be blind, even the poorest vision was a gift to be treasured.

"Miss Solden, have you or have you not completed your homework assignment?" Mr. Lloyd's voice sliced through to her.

The sun went behind another cloud.

"Yes, sir," Anna said, and got out Maggie's map.

Mr. Lloyd walked to her desk and looked down at it. Could he tell somehow that she had not done it herself? She couldn't have done it from the small map in the book, but she planned to make a copy of this larger one tonight so she could learn it. He had told them it was to be one of their test questions on Wednesday. She waited, breath held.

Mr. Lloyd seemed about to speak. Then without a word he turned and walked down the aisle behind her, making acid comments on more than half the maps he was shown, giving detentions to the three boys he caught without the work prepared.

Anna looked across at Maggie again. Maggie smiled. Anna returned the smile, hoping somehow it spoke her thanks.

But that night she took time to make her own map. Something in Mr. Lloyd's silence made doing it herself important. She also made a large outline map she could use for the test, if she just had courage enough to ask.

Two mornings later, when Mr. Lloyd handed out the

pale purple dittoed outline maps on which they were to fill in all the place names, Anna waited till he reached her desk. Then, having rehearsed the one sentence over and over so she could get it out, she said with a dry mouth, "May I use this bigger map, sir, please? I can't see to put the places in on a smaller one. And I need it drawn in black ink."

Again there was an instant of silence while Anna waited. Mr. Lloyd picked up the larger sheet and turned it over. Did he think she had things written in on the back?

"Certainly, Miss Solden," he said.

He returned to the front of the room and stood glaring out over the now-busy class. Anna's hands shook as she filled her fountain pen from her ink bottle. She got out her blotter. She knew the work well enough that she didn't have to use a pencil so she could erase.

Then, as her hand and her heartbeat steadied, she looked up at the teacher.

You're a riddle too, she thought. Why didn't you snap?

She couldn't answer and let it go. Carefully, she printed ST. LAWRENCE RIVER and went on confidently to name the lakes.

11

THE LAST WEDNESDAY in September was the twins'
birthday. As a rule, birthdays were not made much of in
the Solden family, but the twins' had always been an
exception. It was only right that, since there were two of
them, twice as much fuss should be made. Over the years,
it had become a day set aside for a family celebration, an
occasion when not just the twins but everybody had some
special treat. Since it was Fritz's and Frieda's birthday,
their suggestions were given first consideration, and this
time what they wanted to do was first have supper at the
Honeydew Restaurant and second go downtown to

Loews to see *The Wizard of Oz*. It was the last night it would be on.

"It took some coaxing to get Papa to trust the locking up to Mr. Mills," Anna told Maggie at noon on the great day. "He knows the place almost as well as Papa." Mr. Mills did watch repairs at his own house, but he helped out at the store whenever Mama had to miss a day.

"What about his watches?" Maggie asked.

"He says a watch doesn't mind marking time till he can get back to it," Anna quoted. "I think it's really that he likes having a break every so often from working all alone."

"So you're leaving the house about five o'clock," Maggie said, "and making a night of it. I'm so glad you're going to see *The Wizard of Oz*. I loved it—all three times."

Anna folded up the waxed paper which had held her sandwiches. It had started out as a bread wrapper. It was still good enough to be used again.

"I almost feel as though I've already seen it from listening to you," she said. "But being told about a thing ahead of time doesn't spoil it for me. I like to be certain that things will have happy endings before I begin them or I worry too much. It's the first movie I've ever seen in Technicolor. We all had chickenpox when *Snow White* was on. I wanted to see it so badly I thought I'd die."

"You've seen Mickey Mouse cartoons, though," Maggie reminded her. "Not that it's one bit the same because it isn't."

"I'll listen hard and get that one part of 'Somewhere Over the Rainbow' that you missed," Anna said. "Oh, I wish school was over."

When the Soldens came out of the theater, it was dark. Anna had learned the one phrase of "Somewhere Over the Rainbow" that Maggie had not been able to remember and now could sing the whole song.

Once they were off the streetcar and walking the last couple of blocks, she began to sing it. Mama hummed along with her.

Gretchen and Frieda, who were walking out in front, began to sing "We're Off to See the Wizard" in competition.

Then Rudi, not to be outdone, began improvising on the song that the Scarecrow, the Tin Woodman, and the Cowardly Lion had sung. He is as good at improvising parodies as Paula, Anna thought, and stopped singing herself so she could hear his words.

> ". . . I can tell you plump and plain
> I'd be quick on the trigger.
> I could read and write and figure
> If I only had a brain."

"Do the Tin Woodman," Anna said.

"Um . . . let's see," he thought for a moment. "How's this?

> *"If I had a heart like butter,*
> *I'd set all the girls aflutter.*
> *I would play the hero's part.*
> *And then down I would settle*
> *With a miss who's worth her metal,*
> *If I only had a heart."*

There was general applause as he finished.

"Now do the lion," Fritz urged.

"The creative impulse has died," said Rudi grandly.

"Heck," Fritz said. He and Frieda began to talk about the movie.

Anna, a little tired, fell behind. Rudi dropped back beside her and sang very softly, so only she could hear:

> *"If of most things I am wary*
> *And though I find living scary,*
> *Yet the world I'd like to save.*
> *Though my knees would knock and rattle,*
> *I might gladly go to battle . . .*
> *Oh, if only I were brave!"*

Anna looked at him, uncertain how to react. If he meant it lightly, as he had the others, he would have sung the words out for everyone to hear. Was he trying to tell her that he knew he was a coward?

"That's silly," she said aloud. "You're just playacting. How could a boy like you save the world anyway?"

135

He didn't answer but, as they walked under a street lamp, he winked at her.

So he wasn't taking himself seriously! She felt more comfortable. Yet she did not ask him to sing the verse for the others.

One more block and they were home.

It was Gretchen who spied the letter lying on the mat inside the door. She snatched it up before they would trample on it.

"It's . . . I think it's from Aunt Tania, Papa," she said, holding it out to him. "But it's got a Dutch stamp."

Gretchen had a stamp collection, so she should know. Did that, by any chance, mean that Aunt Tania had somehow got out of Germany into Holland? Anna didn't know whether to feel excited or scared. She tried not to feel anything until she knew. Papa reached for the paper knife on the hall table. Nobody moved while he slit the envelope open, pulled out two flimsy sheets of paper, and skimmed the first page. Then, even before he spoke, they knew that Aunt Tania was not safe.

"Let's go into the living room," he said, "and read this together, sitting down. I should tell you right away that the letter was written in August and that Tania is still in Germany."

Even Mama had no remark to make. They moved ahead of him into the living room. Anna sat down on the hassock beside Papa's chair. He had liked having her there, close to him, in the past. When he was tired or discouraged or when she was lonely or hurt, it had comforted both of them. Perhaps this was such a time.

She knew she had been right when, holding the letter up to the light with his right hand, he let his left rest on her shoulder. He began to read:

"3 August 1939

"Dear Ernie,

"I am sure this letter will reach you, as sure as I can be of anything now, but I can't explain how and I have no idea when. I have written to you regularly but I have had only two letters from you in the last six months. I suspect they are not getting through.

"I shall write in English since that is now your language. I have been working as a translator and I have been grateful to be fluent in English since work is hard to find. Father did not dream I would have to earn my own living when he had taught me to play the piano, sing *Lieder,* embroider, and cook fancy dishes!"

"She kept her house beautifully," Mama interrupted but then hushed, waiting for him to read on. Anna wondered if Rudi had caught that part about how good it was to know more than one language. But his face told her nothing.

"The man for whom I worked was in favor with the new regime. We discussed nothing but the work

137

I did. It is best now not to know what anyone else thinks and to confide in as few as possible."

"Aunt Tania has so many friends and loves so much to talk," Gretchen said, as if to herself. "It must be hard for her."

"It would be if she were still in Frankfurt in her old home," Papa agreed. "But she has moved. Listen."

"Since Tobias' death, I have lived in one room near your old school. But the day after tomorrow I am going to live with Tobias' father. His house-keeper, who has been with him for almost half a century, was told last month that she must not work for him any longer. She would not have obeyed, had she had her way, but her son came a week ago and took her away. Mr. Riesmann was relieved because he did not want her to suffer on his behalf. She is not Jewish, although she insists that she feels as though she is, having lived with the Riesmann family for so long.

"Father does need care however. He had a stroke and must walk with a cane. Also he grows more and more forgetful."

Anna, glancing at her mother, was surprised to see her lips tighten and her eyes grow angry.

"Where's Esther?" Klara Solden burst out. "Surely his own daughter should take responsibility for the old man."

"Esther and David and their children went to England while they still had a chance," Papa said, the anger in his voice matching and then mastering that in hers. "She is safe, Klara, like you and me and our children. What would you have her do? Go back?"

"I spoke without thinking," Mama mumbled, picking at a loose thread on her sleeve. "Forgive me, Ernst."

"Your love for Tania is excuse enough," Papa said, gently now, and began again to read:

"Ernst, please understand that it is not just for his sake that I am going to live with him. I need someone to care for and belong to. I'm tired of being alone. We two will be good for each other.

"This letter may sound sad. Yet day-to-day life is not filled only with unhappiness. Children play. Snowdrops bloom. There was the joyous day when I got your letter with the pictures of the children. They seemed so tall! Tell them that I do not forget them."

Gretchen made a choking sound. Papa read on, his voice steady:

"You remember that Mr. Riesmann used to be a fiercely liberal newspaper editor? He has not altered his beliefs and he talks too much. So far, he seems to have been overlooked by the Gestapo, perhaps because he was once popular and he is now very old and frail. He surely can be no real threat to the State. When I am with him, I will try to keep him in more, hoping out of sight will be out of mind. This may be more difficult than it sounds. He is as stubborn as Tobias was.

"He has told me not to come. He has no fear for himself, but he is afraid for me. 'I do not want you,' he says. But we both know he is lying. Together we can talk of Tobias and of the old days and ease each other's loneliness.

"There is so much I want to say but cannot. Whatever happens, Ernie, remember that I know exactly what I am doing and that I am doing it of my own choice.

"Give my love to Klara and to each of the children: Rudi, Gretchen, Fritz, Frieda, and Anna. Just saying your names over to myself gives me pleasure. It comforts me that you are together in a safe place. I pray God's blessing on you daily.

"Don't try to do anything for me no matter what news reaches you. You are so dear to me I could not bear it if you were here.

> "Auf Wiedersehen,
> Your loving Tan"

Papa did not look at anyone as he folded the thin sheets of paper and replaced them in their envelope. He then put it in the breast pocket of his coat.

Rudi spoke first, his voice as deep as a man's.

"Papa, what does she mean at the end when she says 'whatever news reaches you'? Does she mean the war? It sounds as though she knows something bad will happen. How can she?"

Papa's answer came slowly, as though it was difficult for him to get the words out.

"She doesn't know. Not for certain. The old man may attract no special attention. But she doubts this. I do too. He is a brave, outspoken man and too old to change his ways. When we left Germany, free speech was already dangerous. Even more so if you were a Jew, as he is. It is astonishing that he is still left alone."

"Maybe he hasn't talked to the wrong people," Gretchen said, doggedly hopeful. "Maybe they've forgotten all about him."

"If they've forgotten him, why did they make his housekeeper leave?" Frieda asked.

"Tania hoped we wouldn't ask ourselves that question," her father said. Then he looked at Rudi again. "I told you we must laugh, didn't I, son? This letter makes it much harder. Impossible. Tania was saying good-bye. All we can do is pray for her safety, as she prays for ours. And rejoice that we are here 'together in a safe place,' as she says."

"But you can't rejoice, can you, Papa?" Rudi said quietly, as though he were the adult and his father the child. "You want to go back for her."

"If I only could," Papa said.

141

If it weren't for us, Anna thought, he would go and try. Even if he died for it.

She looked up at Rudi. Seeing his expression as he, too, looked at Papa, she was sure he had the same thought.

She tried to think of something to lighten the darkness that seemed to have fallen over them. After all, it was still the twins' birthday. But she could not think of a thing and neither could anyone else. They said "good night" quickly and went away to their beds.

The next morning, Maggie was the only one waiting when Anna arrived at their meeting place. Before Anna could speak, Maggie demanded, "Did you get the part I missed? In 'Somewhere Over the Rainbow'?"

"Yes," Anna said, from what seemed to her a great distance. Yet she was thankful to Maggie. The song would allow her to stop thinking about the sadness at home. She began to sing it:

"Somewhere over the rainbow,
way up high,
There's a land that I heard of
once in a lullaby. . . ."

She stopped.

"I know that much," Maggie said impatiently. "It's the part right after that. . . . Anna, what's wrong?"

"Nothing," Anna said, pulling herself together. "I just was reminded of a lullaby someone used to sing to me

142

when I was little. It was . . . it was about raisins and almonds and a little goat."

Then she hurried on with the song, her voice only wavering on the first two or three words:

> *"Somewhere over the rainbow,*
>   *skies are blue*
> *And the dreams that you dare to dream*
>   *really do come true."*

"That's it," Maggie cried. " 'And the dreams that you dare to dream . . .' I kept singing 'There's a land' again. And I knew it wasn't right. Hi, Paula."

Suzy came running up the next minute and they were on their way.

And soon, Anna found herself laughing at Paula's account of the part she had been given in the Dramatic Society's first play.

"I told you I was the maid. Well, yesterday we got our scripts. I answer the phone once and the door twice. Miss Sutcliff had us read it through and I was putting my all into it and she said, 'Paula, you're not Lady Macbeth. Don't spend five minutes slinking to the phone or they'll have hung up.' I thought maybe today I'd pretend to be hard of hearing and keep asking people to speak up. I have to get some drama out of it or what's the point of being in it at all?"

"You wouldn't? Not really?" Anna said.

"I dare you," Suzy said, knowing Paula.

The three of them went to watch the rehearsal. As Paula began to carry out her plan, they convulsed in stifled laughter. Miss Sutcliff did not allow her to finish, though. She stopped everything and delivered a few stinging remarks about people who could not resist "showing off." Then, still keeping her face straight, she assigned the chastened Paula a different part. The girl who had been given it first was moving away.

"It'll offer you more scope, Paula," the teacher said.

She then dismissed the cast till the following afternoon.

"Which one are you?" Anna demanded as they started to leave.

Paula grinned. "The one who gets poisoned in the first scene," she said.

12

FOR THE NEXT FEW DAYS, Anna found herself thinking
of the letter at the oddest times: while they were shopping
for shoes, when she was struggling with homework, during breakfast, and nearly every night before she fell asleep.
Then, bit by bit, the drama of her own life came between
her and thoughts of Aunt Tania. By the end of October,
it seemed the letter had come years before. They heard
nothing more but they did not expect to. Anna even
caught herself hoping they wouldn't, because she was
afraid of what might have happened since August.

Rudi had now almost disappeared into the world of
University. He was sometimes home for supper but more

often he came in late and ate what Mama had kept warm in the oven for him. He worked long hours in the library.

"He is growing too thin," his mother worried aloud as he hurried out of the house early one Saturday morning, "and he is not happy. Yet he will not talk to me. I ask and he brushes my questions off like flies."

Anna was too busy in her high school life to be much aware of her older brother. He didn't look too thin to her. And Rudi had plenty of reason to be happy, she thought. He was studying all his favorite subjects, and he loved studying.

Then, a couple of days later, she passed him in the hall downstairs and she saw his face suddenly blaze with excitement.

"Oh, I see, I see!" he cried out. "It's so beautiful!"

Anna stood still and watched him rush away up the stairs, his feet stumbling because his eyes were still bent on the book he held in his hands. She had seen enough to know it had something to do with a kind of mathematics completely outside her experience. How could he possibly get excited about anything in a book like that!

Well, Mama's wrong about him being unhappy anyway, she told herself, going up to work on her own homework. She had not known that her mother's words had disturbed her until she felt a sudden relief at seeing that they were not true.

She told Papa about it later. Her father smiled.

"Rudi has a fine mind," he said. "It is wonderful to watch him discovering how to use it, to see it becoming

146

such a joy to him. But you, Anna, how is your math? What are you studying this year? I have trouble keeping everyone straight."

"Algebra," Anna said, looking away. She wished she could ask Papa for aid, but he had often admitted he was no mathematician. Mama kept the books at the store, but she had never studied algebra. Anyway, Mama was like Paula—quick herself but unable to explain to someone else. Rudi, of course, would know all the answers but he seemed so busy, and Anna had never in her whole life gone to him when she was in trouble. He seemed kinder now but preoccupied. And what if he laughed at her! Anna changed the subject. "I love my English teacher, Papa. But I'm having great trouble with French."

"French?" Papa was all interest, algebra forgotten. He spoke French almost as well as he did English. He loved studying languages the way other people loved hockey or chess. "What's wrong?"

"The accent marks in my book are so small. I have trouble making them out and I can't remember them. And Miss Raymond takes off points every time you slant one the wrong way. The circumflexes, too."

"Of course, they must be right," Papa agreed with Miss Raymond. "What if I make you a big dictionary of your vocabulary with all the accents in, big and black? Couldn't you memorize them from that?"

"That would be perfect," Anna said, smiling at him. "Oh, Papa, you're such a help!"

Her father laughed at her but looked pleased and went

to get large sheets of paper and a big black crayon so he could begin. As he worked at it, she came to watch. He looked up.

"Anna, when you want to practice these words, let me help you in the evening. If you say them correctly, you will soon know which accent belongs where."

So French became easier. But algebra was still completely beyond her. The only consolation was that Mr. McNair had not yet discovered how little she knew. She always had her homework done, because she copied Paula's at lunchtime. Thank goodness math was last period in the afternoon!

One day in November, they moved from cooking to sewing in home economics and Anna had to face Miss Marshall and break the news that she could not thread a needle or, once threaded, make small neat stitches with one, and that her parents had forbidden her to use a sewing machine.

"They're afraid I'll sew my finger to something, I guess," Anna said.

Miss Marshall had, of course, realized that Anna's vision was poor but not that poor. She looked flustered momentarily, and angry, as if Anna had invented the problem to make things difficult. Then her frown vanished.

"You can knit!" she announced, obviously pleased with herself for hitting upon a solution so quickly. "Blind people are wonderful knitters."

148

Without giving Anna a chance to express an opinion, the teacher went to the back of the room and rummaged in her cupboards. Before long, she emerged triumphant with a pair of knitting needles and a ball of dingy gray wool.

"Can you cast on?" she asked, coming back to where Anna waited.

Anna shook her head.

"Mama tried to teach me to knit when I was eight," she said, looking and feeling embarrassed, "but I was terrible at it. I do remember how to do the stitches . . . I think."

She was not given a chance to explain that Mama's attempts to teach her had happened before she got glasses, and that, given another chance, she was sure she could learn.

Miss Marshall cast on a row expertly, in a matter of seconds. "There," she said, making it clear that she felt well rid of Anna and her problems. "You just go and knit at that while I get on with showing the class how to begin their aprons."

Anna sighed and started.

"Anna Solden, don't hold your needles like that!" Miss Marshall exclaimed. "Here. Give them to me. Now watch."

Anna tried. She did see that the teacher did not tuck the needles down the way Mama did and did not move only her right hand. But before she had figured out Miss

Marshall's method, the knitting was handed back to her. She laid it down on the table and pretended her shoe needed tying, counting on someone to call the teacher's attention away from her. When she straightened up, sure enough Miss Marshall had moved on to supervise Patsy Rawlings threading the machine.

"How do I have to do it?" she whispered to Maggie.

Maggie arranged the needles in Anna's hands. Knitting had never been easy, but even a simple garter stitch almost defeated her when she could not use her needles in the German way. With Maggie quietly correcting her whenever she went wrong, she persevered.

When the bell rang to end the period, she had produced a very small, very lumpy piece of material. There were two obvious holes in it and it was considerably wider where she finished than it had been when Miss Marshall cast it on.

The teacher took one look, ripped the whole thing out, and said, "Perhaps you will improve with practice."

She sounded as though she doubted it. Anna doubted it even more.

"What use is it?" she complained to the others as they moved to their next class. "She can't be going to make me knit the same piece over and over, can she?"

"I wouldn't put it past her," said Maggie.

"If she'd teach me, I might be able to learn to cast on anyway," Anna said, "but maybe I couldn't either. She doesn't go slowly and she stands too far away."

"Get your mother to teach you," Paula suggested.

"She doesn't do it Miss Marshall's way and she'd never change," Anna said, and gave up.

As they neared the door of Miss Sutcliff's room, she burst out, "I don't see how she can say that blind people are wonderful knitters. It's . . . it's like saying all Negroes are marvelous singers or all Germans are Nazis."

"But, Anna," Suzy said, "I know what you mean, I guess, about Germans. But the Germans in Germany, the real Germans, they're Nazis."

Anna whirled on her.

"They are not!" she cried. "How dare you say a thing like that? Lots of German people—hundreds!—hate what Nazis do!"

"Take it easy, Anna." Maggie, who was the only one Anna had told about Aunt Tania's letter, took hold of her friend's arm and held her back. "Suzy doesn't know what she's talking about. And it's time for English. If you have to fight, do it after."

For once, Anna found it hard to pay attention to what Miss Sutcliff was saying. The period was half over before she had calmed down. It had been a difficult morning but still she was startled by the intensity of her rage, for she had known, really, that Suzy spoke out of ignorance.

But so many people don't know any more than she does, she thought. I guess that's what made me so mad. How can you teach so many?

She looked over at Suzy. The other girl happened to

look across at her at the same moment. She clearly still had no idea of what lay behind Anna's anger. She looked uncertain, even hurt. Anna smiled, repentant. Suzy instantly beamed back.

She's forgiven me, Anna thought ruefully. She knew that she should try to explain to Suzy later on why she had been angry, but she also knew that she wouldn't. Telling Maggie about Aunt Tania was one thing. Telling Suzy would be impossible.

13

ANNA HAD OBSERVED ARMISTICE DAY, or Poppy Day as the children called it, each year since she had come to Canada. It was in honor of the end of the 1914–1918 war. But this year was special because they were at war again.

Still the assembly began much the same as all the others. The Scripture verse was still John 15:13. "Greater love hath no man than this, that a man lay down his life for his friends."

They sang, as always, "Oh, God, Our Help in Ages Past."

The girl who had won last year's grade twelve orator- ical contest recited "In Flanders Fields." Anna, along with every other Canadian child, had had to memorize it long ago. Still she found herself listening with interest.

> *"In Flanders fields, the poppies blow*
> *Between the crosses, row on row*
> > *That mark our place; and in the sky*
> > *The larks, still bravely singing, fly*
> *Scarce heard amid the guns below.*
>
> *"We are the Dead. Short days ago*
> *We lived, felt dawn, saw sunset glow,*
> > *Loved, and were loved, and now we lie*
> > *In Flanders fields.*
>
> *"Take up our quarrel with the foe.*
> *To you from failing hands we throw*
> > *The torch; be yours to hold it high.*
> > *If ye break faith with us who die*
> *We shall not sleep, though poppies grow*
> > *In Flanders fields."*

Anna did not like the last verse as well as the first two. Suddenly she realized that there must be no skylarks in Canada, for she had never heard one here. Or even heard them mentioned. But there were skylarks in Germany, and she remembered how they sang. The day Papa had made her aware of them was, in that instant, as fresh in her memory as though it had happened last week. They had been out in the country, going for a walk, and she had just started to get tired when Papa said, "Listen. That's a lark singing."

The twins had stood, craning their necks back, searching the sky for the bird. Anna, who had never seen a bird in flight, did not bother to look up.

"Where is he, Papa?" Frieda demanded. "I can't see him."

"Larks fly so high they are only specks against the sun," Papa said, "but they keep singing as they mount up. Listen."

And Anna, too, had heard the shrill joyous song falling down to them out of the blue.

Now she said the line about the larks over to herself:

> . . . and in the sky
> *The larks, still bravely singing, fly*
> *Scarce heard amid the guns below.*

A Canadian doctor named John McCrae had written the poem, she knew. Wasn't he supposed to have written it in the middle of a battle, in between caring for wounded soldiers? How could he have noticed larks at a time like that? she wondered, coming on the thought unexpectedly. Most people would have heard only the guns.

Then everyone at the assembly stood while the names of graduates of Davenport Collegiate who had died in that war were read aloud. The students stood for two minutes of profound silence. Then a boy from the band played "The Last Post" on his bugle. He played from behind them, so that the notes floated out over them, beautiful, infinitely sad. Although her father had fought in the wrong army, and not one of the names read out had special meaning for her, Anna felt her heart wrench at the thought of all those young men being killed. After all, they had been boys here, standing in this very hall. They must have wanted to go on living as much as she did.

Then, when they took their seats, the hush still holding, Mr. Appleby came out on the stage and began to talk to them.

"How many of you noticed that the poet, in the middle of a bloody and terrible battle, still could hear the singing of larks? Faintly but still bravely singing. In a sense, that is what I want to talk to you about. How important it is to stay aware of something other than the sounds of gunfire. Wartime is a time of despair and fear and loneliness and loss. Not many of us have had to face those things yet, but before this war is done most of you will have been touched by tragedy. Some of you may well be called on to fight in the armed services. You will all hear of hatred, violence, and slaughter. Some of you may already have experienced special tension— those of you with relatives in the British Isles or in Europe."

He does know, Anna thought. That was why he said

all that about us on the first day of school. He used our family to stand for all the rest, Paula and Carl . . . She cut short her thoughts, not wanting to miss what he was saying.

"You will have to grow up more quickly than any group of students I have ever had before. We are facing a hard time and you are not children to be spared its pain, sheltered from its sorrow."

He paused for a moment. Though hundreds of young people sat facing him, there was not a sound.

He's talking to us as though we matter, Anna thought.

"But you have something special to give to the rest of us in this time of trial. You have faith. Once at a revival meeting, I heard a preacher say, 'Faith is when you hear the bird singing before the egg is hatched.' I thought it so perfect a definition, I have never forgotten it.

"Teachers have that kind of faith in their pupils or they would not be able to teach. They see promise, sometimes when no one else can see it, and over and over, because of their faith, they work hard enough to make the promise come true. Many people have faith in something.

"But I think that *you* must have faith in the whole world. It is going to appear hard and cruel in the months to come, and many of us will lose hope. You, with your young eyes which see more clearly, must look deeper. Keep believing that, somewhere, there is goodness, beauty, joy, love. When you find them, share them with us.

"To me, the world is like that unhatched egg. Older people, embittered by suffering, will tell you that it is rotten, that it is not worth saving. But you must warm the world the way the mother bird warms her egg. Warm it back into life and love. It is terribly important that young people like you listen for the singing.

"Because when this world breaks open, the new world will be yours. And your faith in it and in yourselves will shape the future, will decide whether there will still be a song.

"I am putting this badly. But remember the poet hearing the larks. And the preacher's words, 'Faith is when you hear the bird singing before the egg is hatched.' It is up to you to keep the faith . . . and listen for the singing."

He usually finished off with a joke, but this time he just stopped and looked out over the sea of faces. Anna, looking up at him, wanted to say out loud, "I will. I'll try." The whole student body seemed to be pledging the same thing. Mr. Appleby smiled, said "Thank you" quietly, and dismissed them.

Anna walked out with the others. She felt as though she had made a huge discovery, as though, at last, she understood why she was alive right now, today.

That night, she told Papa about the speech.

"He is a fine man," he said. "Tell me again."

Then he helped her with her French. She did not tell him about the knitting.

In the next few days, Anna tried to hold on to her mood of exaltation but it was hard. Though she tried to think about the war, she still found it impossible. There was still no news about Aunt Tania. And nothing seemed to be happening in the war. Nothing at all.

14

AT THE END OF NOVEMBER, after so many weeks had passed that she had stopped worrying, Mr. McNair found out about Anna and her algebra.

It was all her own fault too.

She had copied Paula's homework for so long that she no longer thought of it as cheating. It wasn't as though it was a test and she was getting good marks for work she hadn't done.

She still never put up her hand, of course. Mr. McNair knew about her poor vision and did not ask her to go to the board. At first, while he called out the names of those who had to go forward and demonstrate in front of the entire class how they had solved a problem, she waited, her stomach fluttering wildly, her eyes fixed on the lid of her desk, and hoped, prayed even, that he would overlook her. Finally, after he had sent the others in her row up four, then five, then six times and left her out, she had relaxed and felt secure. He was not going to bother her. He understood she was different. He was a wonderful man.

So, that gray afternoon, Anna, feeling perfectly safe, turned around in her desk and whispered to Maggie a joke Fritz had told her at breakfast. Maggie, caught off guard, giggled right out loud. And kind, understanding, wonderful Mr. McNair said, "Anna, will you please go to the board and show us how you did problem 17?"

Anna could not believe her ears. She sat where she was, hoping it was a mistake, that he would realize that . . .

"Anna, did you hear me?" her teacher asked. "Or were you too busy talking to Maggie?"

Anna knew then that he meant it.

"Yes, sir," she said, floundering. "I mean, no, sir."

"Then don't keep the class waiting," Mr. McNair said and motioned for her to proceed to the blackboard.

Anna picked up the textbook and stumbled forward to meet her doom. She knew you were allowed to take your text but not your notebook with you. She also knew she had not the slightest idea of how even to begin problem 17. Well, that was not quite true. She did know one sentence.

She picked up the chalk and wrote, her hand shaking, the chalk squeaking with every stroke.

Let X = the unknown quantity.

That much done, she stood there, helpless, the chalk still clutched in her fingers, nothing inside her head.

"Go ahead, Anna," Mr. McNair said.

Anna did not move, remained mute.

"Do you know which problem I asked you to do?"

"Yes, sir."

"Is your homework done?"

Anna nodded.

"Let me see your work."

She returned to her desk. Mr. McNair bent over her notebook. The problem was there, done correctly, exactly the way she had copied it from Paula.

"But. . . ." Mr. McNair began, puzzled. Then he looked straight at her.

"Did you copy these answers from someone else?"

"Yes, sir," Anna said, her face burning.

"Come in after four o'clock."

After school, he tried hard. He asked her when she first did not understand, once he made certain that she had not done her own homework from the beginning. He was so kind that Anna longed to thank him by doing well. He did not even mention cheating. All she could offer in return was honesty about what bewildered her.

"You said, when you subtract, change the minus to a plus and add," she told him.

Mr. McNair stared at her. That had been weeks ago.

"Yes?" he said.

"But you're supposed to be subtracting," Anna said, her voice dogged but hopeless.

She knew she would not understand whatever he said next and she did not. His fingers took up her pencil and worked quick, neat examples for her in her notebook.

"Like this," he said. "Now do you see?"

How could she explain that she could not read his figures and that, even if he made them bigger, she would have to put her face down embarrassingly close to his hand to follow what he was doing? And that what he said still made no sense to her? For why would you add when you were supposed to be subtracting? Why would you?

"Yes, sir. Thank you." Anna said, not knowing what else to do.

"You should ask Rudi for help, Anna," Mr. McNair said. "That boy was the most brilliant mathematics student I ever taught. How is he getting along now?"

"Just fine," Anna said, gathering up her books. "He . . . he likes it!"

The teacher laughed. "Ask him. Maybe he can help you to like it too," he said.

Anna left the school wondering what she should do. Ask Rudi for help? That would mean breaking her years-

163

old habit of avoiding letting him see any chink in her armor in case he used his advantage against her. He so often had when she was smaller. He had been kind lately, true, but who knew what might happen if she told him how algebra had stumped her? How could he, with his brilliant mind, take her problems seriously? She was sure that what baffled her would be so rudimentary to him that he would be unable to believe she could be so stupid.

She hurried a little. It was getting dark. And she had to see Curly on her way. He was a toy poodle and she had adopted him as her own when Mop was finally sold. He was still so tiny and sweet. . . .

Curly was gone. There were no puppies in the window, not one. Just a couple of rabbits, a guinea pig, and three birds hanging in cages. Anna stood there, shivering, feeling as though the sky had caved in on her. It shouldn't matter. This had happened before, over and over. There would be new pups tomorrow or the next day.

But she knew, suddenly, with a sickening jolt of hard fact, that, just as she would never understand algebra, she would never ever have a dog of her own. Never.

She turned and walked away.

When she reached the house, she headed for the kitchen, knowing she was late, knowing Gretchen would be annoyed with her since it was her turn to come home right after four and help.

But Gretchen was not there. Only Rudi sat at the kitchen table. Something in the way he sat there drove all thoughts of puppies and school from her head.

"What is it?" she said. "Rudi, why are you here?"

"I'm waiting for you," he answered, startling her both by the unexpectedness of the words themselves and by the dead quiet of his voice.

"Why? What happened?" Anna cried, growing frightened. "Where's Gretchen? Rudi, what's WRONG?"

"Gretchen and Frieda are upstairs with Mama. Fritz had a game after school. He won't be here till after supper. Papa had to stay at the store. I . . . I was going to wait with Papa, but he sent me home. And then I thought of you . . . and waited," Rudi said.

Anna wanted to shake him, to scream at him to explain. Why was Mama home at all? Why. . . ? Yet she knew that he was doing his best. She did not know how she knew this, but she did. She forced herself to be still and give him time. As she waited, her eyes never left his face, which looked dazed with shock.

"A letter came. Mailed from Switzerland. It was from a neighbor of Aunt Tania's."

Anna felt dizzy. She held on to the table edge and kept on listening.

"They came to arrest Mr. Riesmann. The Gestapo, I guess. The Nazis anyway. The neighbor doesn't say who came. Just 'they.' It was early in the morning. He wasn't even dressed. Aunt Tania went out on the step to argue with them. The neighbors could see and hear but they stayed inside their own houses because they were afraid."

Rudi paused. He had been staring past her as he spoke. Now he looked down at his own right hand.

"I would have been afraid, too," he said very softly.

Anna waited. He began again where he had left off.

"Although Aunt Tania told them he was old and sick and tried to stop them coming in, they paid no attention to her. Just pushed her out of the way and went in and got him. He was still in his dressing gown and slippers.

"Then Aunt Tania ordered them to wait because she was going with him.

"Mr. Riesmann told her to go back in the house. Shouted at her, the letter said.

"But she was so . . . so strong, I guess, that they did what she told them to. She ran in and came out with one suitcase and the old man's cane and spectacles.

"Then they took them away."

Rudi's voice started to shake uncontrollably on the last sentence. He stopped and wiped his hand across his mouth.

"But where did they take her?" Anna cried. "What happened? Rudi, don't stop there!"

"That's all," Rudi said, his voice dead again. "They have not been seen since that morning. The neighbors dared not ask questions. The one who wrote was afraid even to put it into a letter, but she used no names. She called Aunt Tania 'she' and Mr. Riesmann 'the old man.' She wrote because she was a friend of Papa's from when they were children but she didn't sign her name. Papa thinks he knows who she is but he isn't sure. They are just gone, Anna. To prison, to . . . nobody knows. Just vanished."

Rudi stopped talking as suddenly as he had started. Anna stood very straight in the abrupt silence and did not know how she felt or what she should do. Yet, numb with shock, she still, against her will, found herself remembering Gerda Hoffman's father, who had disappeared long before they left Frankfurt and who had never been heard from or seen again.

Then Rudi's head dropped onto his right arm, which lay crooked upon the tabletop. He began to cry. Anna had never seen him cry before, had never imagined him hurt like this. Now she felt herself coming alive to what he had told her, believing it. And she felt that he, as he spoke, must have seen it as clearly as though he himself had been standing there.

Like the neighbor who wrote, she thought. He thinks he would have hidden, too, and not helped.

Even as she thought this, she was shocked most of all by the way he wept. He had always seemed invincible. Now his hand lay stretched out across the table. Almost as if he was reaching out to her!

Anna, after a moment's hesitation, put her hand over his large one. He turned his hand over and they held tightly to each other.

"Poor Papa," Anna said then.

Always, even in an hour like this, unlike any she had experienced before, she thought of her father. If they felt grief, what must he feel?

But then her mind and heart came back to the boy in

front of her. He had waited for her. Rudi had thought of her coming home and waited.

"Rudi," she said slowly, as his wrenching sobs grew quieter, "Rudi, I cannot do algebra."

He looked up at her as though she had spoken to him in Greek, as if he wondered who she was and what the two of them were doing there.

"Rudi," she persisted, unable to stop herself. "I cannot understand why you change the minus sign to a plus and add, when you are subtracting. It makes no sense. To add when you subtract."

He still looked blank. Probably it was so basic that he did not even know what she was talking about. She wished she had kept quiet. Then his expression changed. He thought for a moment. When he spoke, at last, it was not at all what she expected.

"When you play that card game Papa invented, Anna, he always beats you, doesn't he?" Rudi said.

Anna nodded, still holding her brother's hand, although his grip was loosening now.

"When you lose, you get a minus score, don't you?" he asked.

Anna nodded again. Maybe there was some relation but she still saw none.

"When you get two minus scores, how do you figure out what your total score is?" Rudi asked.

"Add them up," Anna said.

"But they are minus scores!" Rudi said, watching her

face. "Minus means subtract, doesn't it, Anna? Yet you change the minus to a plus. . . ."

Suddenly, Anna completely forgot Aunt Tania's disappearance, Rudi's tears, Papa's aloneness. The dark kitchen seemed to grow bright around her.

"I see! I see! Oh, you make it so plain!" she cried. "How could I have missed it?"

Rudi let go of her hand. He smiled at her. He stood up. He seemed taller than he had been.

"You would have figured it out, Anna," he said. "Let's go back to the store. Papa shouldn't be there alone."

They did not talk to each other on the way to the store. Anna felt shy, ashamed of talking about algebra as she had, and yet delighted that something that had worried her for so long had proved to be so easy to understand, with Rudi's help. She wondered if her brother would be sorry he had cried in front of her. She hoped not. He seemed different now—ever since the war started. Sometimes he seemed to be not the big brother she had learned to mistrust and avoid but a person who might almost be a friend.

Papa was alone in the store. Neither Rudi nor Anna was surprised. Quite a few customers bought their groceries somewhere else nowadays, not wanting to deal with Germans. Now that weeks had gone by and nothing much more seemed to be happening overseas, some were shamefacedly drifting back.

"I'm closest," Papa explained it. "But they will remember I am German again when Canadians begin getting killed."

"How is Klara?" he asked, as they came in.

Rudi let Anna answer. Just before they left, she had run up to check and to tell Gretchen they were going. Mama was lying down, sobbing noisily.

"If Tania had only listened!" Anna had heard her wail. "Ernst tried to tell her. I argued with her myself. And why did she need to go to that old man? How could she help? She should have let them take him. She will get herself killed for nothing!"

"She's resting," Anna said. Papa would probably guess she was not resting quietly.

It was strange how Mama seemed to have forgotten that she herself hadn't wanted to move to Canada, that she had begged to stay behind as Aunt Tania was doing.

Papa smiled wearily, put out one hand to cup Anna's cheek, and then started counting up the money in the till. It looked like quite a lot. Mostly change though. Hardly any bills.

Rudi began to help, his fingers quick, never pausing in his adding. Watching him Anna thought of something to cheer her father.

"I understand now why you change a minus to a plus and add, Papa," she said. "Rudi explained. Mr. McNair told me to ask Rudi for help. He said, 'Rudi is the finest mathematics scholar I ever taught.'"

Papa paused and looked from his daughter to his tall son.

"I am glad your fine mind is a help to your sister," he teased. Rudi's head jerked up and the handful of change he was counting rattled and rang on the countertop.

"Papa, I am eighteen!" he cried. "And the world is at war! And all I can do is help Anna with the simplest thing in her schoolwork. What use am I?"

"It didn't seem simple to me," Anna muttered, picking up quarters.

"Rudi, the world is not yet at war. Not really. On the brink, yes. And it will come. But the best thing an eighteen-year-old boy with a fine mathematical mind can do at this moment is to train that mind further so that he can be of use when the time comes. For weeks now you have been wondering where your duty lies, I know. A couple of your classmates have enlisted, I imagine."

"Only one really," Rudi said, with a sudden grin. "Ike tried but he has flat feet. How do you like that for a reason for not going to war? He would never have told except that we all knew he was going into the army."

"Anyway," Papa said, smiling at the digression but not led astray by it, "what use would you really be at this time, Rudi? Canada has become your country, true, and when she needs you perhaps you will have to go. But Klara is your mother and she needs you now more than Canada does."

Rudi whirled on him, all the laughter gone from his face.

"What about Aunt Tania?" he cried. "Mama is safe enough. Who is helping Aunt Tania?"

Anna was surprised to see her father smile again, even though this was a wry smile with amusement in it but no mirth.

"At this very minute, I expect Tania is taking care of herself better than anyone else could," he said. "Since she was little more than a baby, my sister has been standing up to people and getting her own way. She is a deeply loving person, sometimes too loving, if such a thing is possible, but extremely headstrong. As Mutti used to say, 'If Tania decides to help you, she will help you, whether you want help or not.' If it is possible for her to survive, she will fight to do so."

He took a deep breath. Anna wished she was not there. Yet she was not bothering them. They hardly seemed to notice her.

"Don't misunderstand me, Rudi. I am desperately afraid for her. But she herself told us what we were to do when this happened. Didn't you understand her message? 'Don't try to do anything for me, no matter what news reaches you.' "

As he repeated his sister's words, his hand moved slightly as if to take the envelope out of his coat pocket, and in that instant, Anna knew, as surely as if he himself had told her, that he carried the letter with him always and that he had read it over until he knew the whole thing by heart.

"Yes, I'm sorry, Papa," Rudi said.

Anna understood how inadequate he felt and why he

turned away from Papa and began counting the money again. Their father walked away from them and busied himself for a few moments rearranging something on one of the shelves. When he came back, the anguish had left his face and he was himself again.

"Part of the torment you are putting yourself through is simply because you are ashamed of being German, isn't it?" he said quietly. "Maybe some of the others have said cutting words . . . or no words at all. Am I right?"

Rudi nodded. Then he lifted his head and faced Papa.

"It's not just that I'm ashamed. That might be easier. It is partly that I still care about people in Frankfurt. Mrs. Gimpel who made us the gingerbread. Dagmar Berger. I had a crush on her. What are the boys I knew doing, Papa? Helmut was nearly two years older than the rest of us. Did he fight in Poland? Such questions come hammering at me all the time, even in school. Twice I've almost answered a question in German and just caught myself in time."

"You have to be stronger than this, son," Papa said. "I, too, could let thoughts of those we left behind haunt my every moment. But we have work to do, both of us."

"Work," Rudi said with scorn, as though his studies were beneath contempt.

"Work," Papa repeated. "And an important part of your work is helping Anna. If Hitler and his henchmen had been taught to care for and serve those weaker than themselves, to protect rather than to destroy . . ."

He stopped short. Anna, watching him, wondered. Did his own words make him remember himself helping his younger sister with something? Anna had always loved hearing stories of when her parents were children. Especially Papa's stories because he made the past live again as he spoke of it. But this was not the time to ask.

Or was it?

If it were a happy memory, maybe it would heal more than it would hurt.

She stepped closer to him, so close that she could touch the rough material of his coat sleeve. Then she spoke quickly, before she had time to lose courage.

"Was Aunt Tania good at schoolwork? Or did you have to help her, Papa?"

"She was smarter than I in school in everything but languages," he said. "But she could not learn to ride a bicycle. She wanted to. She had one. But she could not balance. Hours and hours I ran beside her, trying to keep her from toppling over."

"Did she learn?" Anna's face was eager with interest as she pictured the two children she had seen in old brown photographs.

"One day, she just took off like a bird," Papa said, wonder at it still in his voice, "and she shouted back to me, 'Oh, it's easy, Ernst. You never told me it was so easy!'"

"Exactly the way I felt when Rudi told me about us playing cards and going into minus scores," Anna said. "I couldn't believe it was as simple as that."

"There are a few more things you'll have to learn yet, Anna, before you take off like a bird," Rudi said.

Anna, pretending to be affronted, held her head high.

"I have faith in myself," she answered. "Mr. Appleby told us, 'Faith is when you hear the bird singing before the egg is hatched.'"

"I would hatch the egg first and be sure," Rudi mocked her gently.

"I . . ." Anna paused, searching for the right words, the words Mr. Appleby himself had used, "I would listen for the singing."

"Sometimes it will be very hard to hear, Anna," Papa said. "But keep that faith. Come, let's close the store even though it is fifteen minutes early. We should be at home together. Your mother will be worrying."

As Anna watched her father lock the door, she saw he had grown stooped. Why, she was up to his shoulder.

Frightened, she turned away and found Rudi's eyes on her.

"It's all right, Anna," he said, and pulled her hand through the crook of his elbow.

He did not explain what he meant. Perhaps he did not know himself. But walking home between the two of them, holding on to both, Anna felt comforted.

15

"ANNA, CONCENTRATE!" Rudi said sharply.

Anna sighed, leaned her forehead on her hand, and thought that learning algebra wasn't like Aunt Tania flying away on her bicycle, calling back, "Oh, it's so easy!" It was much more like all those hours Papa had talked of when he had run beside her, yelling orders at her that she just couldn't make work.

"Start again," Rudi said. "I don't think you have that first step clear."

"I can't," Anna said, putting down her pencil with a little click and watching as it rolled away across the table.

She made no move to catch it. Rudi scooped it up just as it reached the far edge.

"What's the matter with you? If you don't want to learn, I have better things to do with my time, no matter what Papa says."

Anna had not seen that scornful look in Rudi's blue eyes for a long time but she recognized it. He thought she was a Dummkopf. But it was just that she was worried about something. And she couldn't explain because there was nothing he could do to help.

"I'll give you one more chance," Rudi said in a cold, slow voice. "Either you tell me what's on your mind and why you've stopped learning anything, just when I was . . ."

He stopped and drew a deep breath.

"When you were what?" Anna asked, curiosity breaking through her despair for a moment.

"Well, you were learning so fast, that's all. I was proud of you. You could come out top of your class. But now you don't want to bother so I won't bother either."

He stood up. She had let her one chance slip. Self-pity engulfed her as he began to pick up his things. Then, before she could stop herself, the truth came out of her mouth.

"It's not that I don't want to learn. It's . . . it's the dance."

"Dance?" Rudi echoed, no sympathy as yet in his ice-blue eyes.

"Our grade is having a Christmas dance next Friday night," Anna said, miserably. "They've had tea dances after four and a class dance, and lots of the kids went but I can't dance so I just didn't. Lots of times Maggie didn't either. Paula and Suzy went every time."

"So?" Rudi said, sitting down again.

"Everybody's going to this one. Some of them will be in couples, although most won't. But even Maggie is going. And she's at me and at me and AT me to go, too. Then Suzy said . . ."

Anna's voice broke off. She swallowed.

"Said what?" prompted her older brother mercilessly.

"I don't mean to be mean," she said, "and she didn't either. Suzy does say mean things, but she doesn't think how they make people feel. . . ."

Gretchen had drifted into the room and had now come close enough to listen. Anna put her head down on her arms so they couldn't see her face. Why had she told? Why?

"What did Suzy actually say?" Rudi demanded.

"Oh, Rudi, don't," Gretchen protested. "It's all right, Anna. You don't have to tell."

"If we're going to help her, she does so," Rudi said. "Don't be so soft, Gret."

Anna found herself straightening up, responding to Rudi's blunt good sense.

"She said I couldn't help my looks but nobody would

want to dance with me and I'd hate the whole thing, so since I can't dance, why tell me I should go?"

"We can fix that last part," Gretchen said. "I heard Frieda teasing Fritz because he hasn't learned to dance and he's always on the outside. We could run a dancing class, Rudi. Tomorrow night maybe."

"No, now," Rudi said, making the decision for all of them. He might be kind but he was still eldest and the boss. "We'll push back the sliding doors and make the living and dining rooms into one big room. We can shove everything that'll move up to the far end of the dining room and that'll give us lots of space. You get the twins. Come on, Anna."

Anna sat where she was. He grinned down at her.

"Listen, kid, I'm a terrific dancer," he bragged. "I don't think I missed going to a dance in all my high school years. Also, I have you down on my schedule. Teach Anna. So if you can't learn algebra, we'll try dancing instead. Move."

Anna grew more and more uneasy as she helped him clear everything but the chesterfield out of the living room. Then they rolled back the carpet. Frieda came running with her records. Gretchen came with a loudly protesting Fritz.

"Whose idea was this?" he bellowed.

Mama, who had come to investigate the noise, set a chair for herself in a corner. She looked happier than Anna had seen her in days. Papa, his newspaper

179

only half read, stood leaning in the doorway, watching.

"Rudi, I can't learn," Anna cried, as anxious as Fritz not to be made a fool of. "I'm Awkward Anna, remember? In dancing. In P.T."

"They don't know a thing about it in P.T.," Gretchen said, "especially Miss Willoughby. She's too fat and too slow."

Then Frieda put the first record on and music filled the room. Gretchen grabbed Fritz. Rudi came over to where Anna sat, clutching the seat of her chair with both hands.

"Hey, you're the one with faith," he said. "You were going to listen for the singing before eggs hatched. Well, right now you're about to hatch. Come on."

But she was awkward at first. It was harder than algebra. Rudi teased her till she relaxed and soon he had her moving more and more in time to the music. There was a pattern to it. And his hands showed her which way to move.

Gretchen groaned over Fritz. "Listen to the beat, you big lump," she scolded.

"Anna, you're perfect," Rudi said.

She tripped over his foot, but he caught her deftly and had her dancing again before she had time to blush.

"Nearly perfect, I should have said," he amended.

Then it was time to break for a rest.

"Papa, Mama," Frieda said. "It's your turn." And she put on a polka.

"No, no," Papa protested, trying to back out of the room.

"Come on, Ernst," Mama said, catching him by the hand.

It would have been better if they'd had more room, but they managed. Anna felt a sudden huge love for this roomful of people, her family. Rudi was so smart. She turned to tell him but he had stepped onto the floor and taken Mama away from Papa.

"Sorry, Papa, but she needs a real partner," he said.

And the two of them danced around the living room and out into the hall.

When the furniture was back in place and it was Anna's bedtime, Rudi said to her, "How long before this dance of yours?"

"Three days," Anna answered, feeling sick to her stomach again.

"You'll be able to dance any step any kid can throw at you by then, I promise," Rudi said.

"If anyone asks her," Fritz put in.

He stumbled off up the stairs. Anna, hearing his words like a judge's sentence, knew nobody would ask her. But Rudi had tried.

"Knowing that I could dance, if I were asked, will make it much easier, Rudi," she said. "I'll tell Maggie I'll go. She was going to make me anyway, just to show Suzy."

"I'm glad," Rudi said; yet his face was troubled as he looked down at her.

Half an hour later, he came up to her alcove.

181

"Meet me after school tomorrow night," he said, sticking his head around one end of the curtain, "on the corner by that big spruce."

"What for?" Anna asked.

"Never mind. Just be there."

When she was waiting to fall asleep, she heard him talking to Gretchen, on the stairs. His voice was lowered at first. Then she heard him grow insistent.

"Listen, I'm serious," he said. "I need advice."

"Hush. They'll hear," Gretchen said. She must mean Mama and Papa. "I don't want to be to blame, that's all. I see what you mean, but Mama would kill me. If you do it, it'll be different. But I'll tell you where to go."

Their voices dropped again. Anna was far too tired to wonder what they were discussing. She did not even read before she fell asleep.

She dreamed she was in a huge empty hall and a prince, on a white horse, came riding in.

"You should leave your horse outside," she told him.

She saw, with no surprise, that it was Rudi.

"Can you dance yet?" he asked.

Then she was a bird, flying somewhere very far, and the prince was gone.

I'm lost, she thought. I'm lost.

But she kept on flying.

Then Aunt Tania was flying beside her.

"You see, Anna, it's easy," she said. "I told you it would be."

And Anna knew a surge of joy because Aunt Tania looked so happy, flying comfortably along.

"But you haven't wings," Anna said suddenly.

"I use faith," Aunt Tania said.

Anna turned over, breaking the dream by half waking. Drifting into deeper sleep, she smiled in the darkness.

16

RUDI WAS THERE BEFORE HER, his hands shoved deep into his overcoat pockets, his head bare in spite of the cold December wind. Anna ran up to him, Maggie, Suzy, and Paula close behind her. Except for Maggie, they had never seen Rudi, only listened to Anna boast about him. Suzy had stated openly that she doubted he could be as good-looking as Anna said he was. Paula had said nothing but Anna knew she also doubted it, even though Maggie backed Anna up.

"See!" she said to them triumphantly, as Rudi turned to face them.

"Wow!" Suzy said.

Anna glowed. She introduced her friends. Rudi was

polite but distant. When he had said "Hello," he took Anna by the elbow.

"So long, girls," he said. "Anna and I have an appointment."

"An appointment? Where?" Suzy called after them.

Rudi, practically shoving Anna down the snowy street, pretended he had not heard.

"Rudi, slow down. I'm out of breath," Anna complained a few moments later.

She too wanted to know where they were going but she didn't want to sound anything like Suzy. Rudi would surely tell any minute.

He slowed down but he didn't explain.

Then they were at a street filled with stores. Rudi stopped. Anna kept going a step or two before she realized he had.

"We're going in here," Rudi said, his voice strained.

Anna looked up and gasped. It was a hairdresser's. She had never in her entire life been inside one. It was called Pierre's.

"What for?" Anna said.

"Because you're going to get your hair cut. Cut and curled!" he said. "And Papa and I decided that it should be done properly."

"But Rudi!"

"Don't you want to look right? Are you too scared to try something new for once? Do you want to be the only girl at the dance with braids like that?"

"No," Anna said. The word exploded out of her. She

didn't know which she felt most, frightened, bullied, or excited.

"You couldn't go in by yourself, could you?" Rudi asked, betraying himself.

"Who's scared now?" Anna taunted, feeling stronger at once. "This isn't my idea, it's yours. Come on!"

They were brave words but, if he did desert her, she did not see how she could go in alone. He grinned at her then and, grabbing her firmly by the elbow, propelled her ahead of him into the carpeted, different-smelling, completely foreign place.

"Yes?" said a perfumed, sophisticated, perfectly groomed personage.

Rudi stood helpless before her.

"We have an appointment," said Anna. She was amazed at herself.

"The name?"

Rudi had turned over the responsibility totally. His admiring look gave her the courage she needed to see the thing through.

"Solden," she said coolly. Then, growing positively reckless, she asked, "Will we have to wait long?"

"I believe Antoine can take you at once," the receptionist said, as though Anna was an old customer, and ushered her into a curtained-off booth, where she was seated, confronting endless images of herself caught in the triple mirror. Rudi, looming behind her, looked out of place in the small cubicle. Once the intimidating woman had left them to wait for Antoine though, he became more himself.

"You'd think you'd been doing this all your life," he murmured, looking at her reflection. "I thought you were scared."

"I am," Anna said, her poise vanishing. "Oh, Rudi, why did you bring me?"

Antoine's arrival saved Rudi from having to begin his pep talk all over again. The two of them studied Anna's appearance as it was revealed in the mirror.

"Hmmm," Antoine said, not giving anything away. Rudi and Anna watched him as he undid the thin braids, brushed the wispy brown hair till it stuck out like a dandelion gone to seed, shook his head over it, and muttered in a deep voice, "It is a problem, yes."

Rudi took charge again, to Anna's relief.

"Can you cut it and curl it so she looks like other girls?" he said, coming straight to the point.

Anna felt her cheeks flushing. Maybe it was because of all the lights around the mirrors. She waited, breath held, for the verdict.

"She will look like a princess," Antoine said, sounding almost convincing. "A little beauty. Can you come back for her at about seven o'clock?"

"I'll be here," Rudi promised. He started to back out. Then he paused.

"Good luck," he said.

Knowing he was leaving, Anna could not answer. He

187

ducked out of sight. She swallowed. Then she lifted her chin a little, held very still, and waited for Antoine to begin.

The hairdresser set to work, humming under his breath. Anna watched, fascinated, as bits of her hair were snipped off, fell to her shoulders, slid to the floor. Suddenly, she had bangs. She wished so much that she could see better. She thought maybe they looked wonderful. But they kept flying up to the comb in an alarming way.

Right then, Antoine said, "Let us take off these glasses. They are in the way. Ah, that is better, yes."

Anna had no idea. From that moment until it was over, the whole long process remained a mystery to her. She went where they led her. They washed her hair with a lovely-smelling shampoo. Mama made her use plain soap. They seemed to be coating it with something thick and cold. She sat ramrod-stiff while they did it up on what felt like small metal rods. They dabbed at all the rolls of hair with something that smelled terrible. Then they attached her to a machine and she could feel it cooking her hair. Before Antoine came back, she was sure it was overdone. There was a distinct smell of burning. But he seemed to notice nothing.

He led her back to the mirror, put something else wet on, pinned her hair up, and left her to dry under another machine. Then he brushed and combed and arranged things just so, still humming but in a rather worried tone.

Finally she heard Rudi's voice asking if she was ready.

"Almost the princess is here," Antoine said in a jolly voice. He put the glasses back on her nose and Anna, half horrified, half delighted, beheld her new self.

She was not a princess. But neither was she the old Anna. Her hair looked stiff. It curled all over. She even had curly bangs. It was perhaps a bit *too* curly. Bushy almost? She looked up at Rudi.

"Will it lie down a bit in time?" Rudi asked Antoine.

"Certainly, certainly. It is always just a wee bit artificial at first."

It isn't braids, she reminded herself, getting up out of the chair. It isn't European and old-fashioned, she thought, doing her best to rejoice.

Rudi paid without saying anything more.

They went out together. Anna felt like a new person and she was afraid of herself. What would Mama say? Suzy? Fritz? Papa?

"Don't worry," Rudi said gently. "It'll be all right. We're just not used to it. You really do look more like the others now."

Mama cried. "What have they done to your beautiful hair!" she wailed.

Anna laughed for the first time since she had walked into the hairdresser's.

"Beautiful hair! Mama, you always said I had impossible hair."

"Well, it sure looks different now," Fritz said, eyeing her warily.

"Don't worry, Anna," Gretchen soothed, looking worried herself. "I can fix it. And it will soon grow out."

Anna turned to Papa. If Papa looked at her as though she were a stranger, the way the others did, she was not going to be able to bear it.

He held out his arms.

She ran into them, hiding her face on his shoulder, afraid she might cry. But she didn't. He put his hand gently on the tight curls. "It's hard growing up," he said, close to her ear. "But you are still my Anna."

That night, they danced again. Anna, growing more and more adept at the steps Rudi was teaching her, became used to the new light feeling of her head.

In the morning, her hair was frizzy. It stood out all over her head in a wild bush. Gretchen did her best with it. Fritz advised her to wear a hat and Frieda flew at him, furious on Anna's behalf. Then, because it had to be done, Anna went to school.

They shrieked when they saw her, Suzy especially.

"Oh, Anna, it's a scream!" she cried. "I've never seen such a bushy perm."

"It's marvelous!" Maggie said, patting Anna's arm comfortingly.

"Marvelous isn't quite the word I would have chosen," Paula said, laughter in her eyes. "It's unique! That's the exact word for it."

"I hate it," Anna said, blushing. "It looks *awful*. You don't have to tell me. I saw myself in the mirror."

But she didn't hate it. Not really.

"It's loads better than those braids anyway," Maggie said.

"I think so too," Anna said. "It was Rudi's idea."

That fact still astonished and pleased her. If it weren't for Rudi, none of the family would have become involved in getting her ready for the dance.

On the night of the dance, Gretchen loaned her her only pair of silk stockings, threatening to throttle her if she snagged them. Anna was a little worried but it was worth it. Usually she wore lisle stockings, thick and warm, hitched to her garter belt. The silk ones had no warmth in them at all, yet they made her feel elegant. Suzy would have silk ones, of course, but she was pretty sure most of the others wouldn't.

Frieda carefully applied natural nail polish to her sister's fingernails. Mama said, "No lipstick!" but Gretchen persuaded her to let her put on a very little bit and a touch of face powder. Anna knew Mama would make her wash it off if Gretchen put on the least bit too much but Gretchen knew Mama too. Anna passed inspection safely. Her hair was much more normal than she thought it would be and she did like the bangs. Looking at herself in the mirror, just before she set out with the other girls, Anna felt almost beautiful.

But in the gym, she came down to earth with a thud. As Fritz had prophesied, nobody asked her to dance. Suzy had lots of partners. Eventually, Maggie and Paula, after

191

dancing with each other for a while, were sought out by two or three of the boys from their class.

Anna stood well off the dance floor, in a shadowed corner by a row of lockers. At first she felt safely inconspicuous, but as the minutes passed she began to think everyone noticed her skulking there. Her feet grew heavy and hot, as though they were pushing roots out through her shoes and anchoring her to the floor. She checked to see if the seams up the back of Gretchen's stockings were still straight. They were. She went and got a drink at the water fountain. She returned to her place. Her face burned. She wished it were over.

"Anna, may I have the pleasure of this dance?"

Mr. McNair was standing waiting. A teacher!

"You dance, don't you, Anna?" he asked, his voice kind and steadying.

"Yes," Anna told him. "I do."

And she didn't trip once.

17

ANNA AWAKENED ON SATURDAY, after the dance, and faced a fact that she had been avoiding. On Monday, she was due to begin writing her Christmas exams. Although she was halfway ready, she had not asked anyone about how she was going to be able to read the questions. On regular tests, teachers had trusted Maggie enough to allow her to whisper to Anna the questions on the board. But these examinations were finals. From them came most of your Christmas marks, except in subjects like P.T. She was quite sure that any whispering would be frowned upon.

She first considered approaching Mr. Appleby, feeling

sure she could make him understand. But when she thought of facing the secretaries in the outer office and asking for an appointment, she couldn't make herself. Maybe Mrs. Schumacher could phone him and tell him about the way she always typed exams out on a primer-type typewriter and, Anna hoped, Mr. Appleby might even allow her to do the same thing now. Nobody would dream of not trusting Eileen Schumacher.

"All right," Mrs. Schumacher said when Anna had explained. "Isobel's vision is just that much better than yours that she could manage, but I can see that you have a real problem. I'll call him at home right now. Why on earth did you leave it so late?"

"I don't know," Anna said, shamefaced.

"Well, I'd better phone Mr. Appleby now before it's too late."

Anna listened and heard Mrs. Schumacher begin to explain. Then she broke off, a look of surprise on her face, thanked the principal and hung up.

"It's all taken care of," she said, as startled as Anna. "He said a teacher pointed out your problem at the last staff meeting and offered to type out all your examination papers on a primer-type typewriter exactly as I did. And it's been done. They're ready for you. Are you ready for them?"

"I will be," Anna declared, "but I'd better go home and cram. It must have been Miss Sutcliff. . . . Mr. McNair might have . . . No. I'm sure it was Miss Sutcliff. I'll have to go thank her."

On Monday afternoon, with two examinations over and, she thought, passed, Anna went to Miss Sutcliff's classroom. She waited while the teacher dealt with a couple of other students.

"Did you want to see me, Anna?" she asked then.

Anna smiled at her, feeling shy.

"I came to thank you," she said.

"Well, that's lovely," the teacher answered, "but for what?"

Anna felt embarrassed. Hadn't Miss Sutcliff known that she would guess?

"For typing out the exams in big print."

Miss Sutcliff looked steadily at Anna.

"Thank you for thinking I was the one who was kind enough to think of that," she said, "but it was Mr. Lloyd, Anna. Once he made the suggestion, we all realized that you would have had difficulty; but he not only drew our attention to you, he typed the papers for all of us. It must have taken him quite some time. How many examinations are you writing?"

"Nine," Anna said, grateful that Miss Sutcliff had gone on talking long enough for her to regain her composure. "I . . . I guess I'd better go and thank him then."

"That would be a very nice thing to do," Miss Sutcliff answered. "Have a happy holiday, Anna. It's been a joy having you in my class."

"Me too," Anna said incoherently. "Merry Christmas."

Then she was back in the hall and wondering what to do next. Maybe she should leave it till another day. There was no real reason to thank him right now. Maggie was waiting at the locker. She'd better go and tell her anyway. Maybe, just maybe, Maggie could be persuaded to come with her and help her get it over with.

"Mr. Lloyd?" Maggie said.

"That's just how I felt. I still can't believe it except I know Miss Sutcliff wouldn't lie. Come with me, Maggie."

"I'll wait outside the door and pick up the pieces when you come out," Maggie offered.

"Oh, come on with me. I'm scared."

"I'd be petrified," Maggie said.

They walked to 9E together. Maggie flatly refused to come farther than the open door. Mr. Lloyd had no students waiting to talk with him. But he did not look up till Anna was right beside his desk.

"Yes," he said, his expression as cold as usual.

"I came to thank you," Anna said, all in a rush, her cheeks scarlet. "For typing out the exams so I can read them. I mean, I was really worried and I didn't know what to do and Miss Sutcliff told me you were the one. . . ."

The words dried up in her mouth. She stood where she was, as helpless as a fish on a hook, unable to go, unwilling to stay.

"I had not intended that you know," he said, his voice crisp and dry. "You are welcome, Miss Solden. I'm glad to have helped."

He did not sound glad, and yet he had suggested it

and done all the work of his own free will. Why? How had he guessed . . . ? Her eyes dropped to the desk in front of him. His notebook lay open before him. She had never seen inside it before. The notes were typed in primer type. She stared.

He coughed, made a quick movement as if to close the book, and then left it as it was. His voice lowered slightly, although it still was not warm.

"I share your problem, as you have discovered. I have been interested to see you managing as well as you have. I myself was privately tutored during my high school years. College was much easier because the teaching was done through lectures. Like yourself, Miss Solden, I acquired a better-than-average memory."

"Oh," Anna said lamely. "I never thought . . . Sir, thank you very much for understanding."

He stood up suddenly, pushing back his chair as he did so.

"I admire courage wherever I find it," he said, still with no hint of a smile. "You should go far, Miss Solden. I believe you have a good mind."

"Thank you," Anna said again. Then gathering up the courage he had mentioned, she gave him her warmest smile, held out her hand, and said firmly, "Merry Christmas, sir."

He looked at her hand. Then he shook it quickly as though that was an unpleasant duty he had to perform. But she saw, in that instant, that he did not mean it to be that way. He was almost paralyzed with shyness and he did not know how to be friendly.

"Merry Christmas," he said.

Maggie, who had heard only the last exchange, came rushing up, her eyes wide.

"How did you ever have the nerve?" she gasped.

Anna could not answer.

18

WINTER PASSED. Anna grew used to having curls. In time, they did calm down, as Antoine had promised. Before long, even the night of the dance seemed far behind her.

One afternoon in the middle of March, when the gang was walking home from school, the girls had to stop and wait while some soldiers marched by. The men were chanting as they marched:

> "*Left, Left!*
> I had a good job and I . . . *left!*
> First they hired me;

Then they fired me.
Then, by golly, I . . . *left!*"

Each time they said the word "left," they stepped forward with their left foot. All, that is, but one soldier right at the back. He didn't seem to care. He had his head high, his cap on at a jaunty angle. His hair was the color of straw. Like Rudi's.

"He should switch feet and get back in step," Suzy said, watching him.

"I've never been able to do that," Anna admitted.

"It's simple," Suzy said, her voice just touched with scorn.

Anna felt her cheeks grow hot and was angry at herself, but Suzy was still intent on the soldiers.

Suddenly, the out-of-step one began to sing and, almost immediately, the rest had joined in. The girls, instead of moving on, stood looking after them and listening.

"I've got sixpence, jolly, jolly sixpence.
I've got sixpence to last me all my life.
I've got sixpence to spend
And sixpence to lend
And sixpence to send home to my wife, poor wife!
No cares have I to grieve me,
No pretty little girls to deceive me.
I'm as happy as a lark, believe me,
As we go rolling, rolling home. . . ."

The platoon rounded the corner and disappeared from sight although their song still drifted back to the girls.

"He sure was good-looking!" Suzy said, with an exaggerated sigh. "He didn't look all that old either."

"He'd have to be at least eighteen and that's a little too advanced even for you, Suzanne Hughes," Maggie said. "He didn't even know we were here. He's probably engaged."

"Married, most likely," Paula put in, laughing at Suzy's pouting face. "You know what? I meant to tell you before but I forgot. My cousin joined the army last weekend. He said he just couldn't wait any longer, even though he's only turned twenty and not even halfway through college. My Uncle Edward was fit to be tied but there wasn't a thing they could do."

They crossed the street while she was talking and started up the stretch that led to their homes. Anna, her feet moving along automatically, heard bits and pieces of things they had just said sounding again in her mind.

"He'd have to be at least eighteen."

"He said he just couldn't wait any longer."

". . . not even halfway through college."

When the news about Aunt Tania had come, Rudi had seemed tortured, wanting to stay in school and yet feeling a need to prove himself by enlisting. She had overheard more than one conversation between him and Papa, had seen for herself how tense he was. But just as she had begun to grow anxious, he had become more relaxed. He

201

seemed to have accepted Papa's counsel. As the winter wore on, he grew more absorbed in his studies and also in tutoring her. Where she had before felt close only to Papa, she more and more came to depend on Rudi's friendship.

He cares about me too, she thought.

Was the peace in her home in danger? Suzy's father was predicting that the war would be over by May, but Papa and Maggie's father, and Paula's father too, all felt that when spring came the real fighting would begin.

"Anna, I can teach you to get back in step if you want," Suzy offered, breaking in on her panic. "It's easy. Look."

Anna started to explain she didn't think she could see, but Suzy, every so often, showed more perception than they credited her with. She had grown to understand, over the months, what it took to teach Anna, and as she moved, she talked, describing exactly what she was doing.

Then it was like the historic day when Rudi had first helped her to penetrate the mysteries of algebra. In no time flat, she realized what Suzy meant. Trying it out for herself, she found that she could do it with no trouble at all.

They practiced then, all starting out together on the same foot, marching along in step for eight or ten strides and then, on Suzy's command, all switching over at once.

Then Anna, who picked up things by memory most quickly, began to recite:

> *"Left! . . . Left! . . .*
> I had a good job and I . . . *left*.
> First they hired me;
> Then they fired me.
> Then, by golly, I . . . *left!"*

They had to skirt frequent puddles, for the March sidewalk, though free of snow after a thaw, was still very wet. But it was fun!

When Anna left them, after standing at the corner for an extra half hour talking, she went on marching in step and then changing, pretending she was that young soldier who had started the singing and that one of the others had just taught her how to get back in step, once you were out. A moment later, she found herself singing the words the soldiers had sung.

> *"No cares have I to grieve me,*
> *No pretty little girls to deceive me.*
> *I'm happy as a lark, believe me . . ."*

The song stopped in her throat. Her feet slowed to a walk. It was not a game, being a soldier. How could they sing like that? They were leaving home. They were going away, maybe . . . maybe to be killed.

"Don't let Rudi go," she whispered suddenly to God, to whatever power might be listening. "Don't let him. Please!"

When she went into the house, everything was normal.

She pulled off her rubbers and hung up her coat, leaving her mittens stuffed in the pockets, and went to help get supper. As she peeled hard-boiled eggs, sliced meat, went down cellar for a jar of preserved plums to help Frieda, and then set the table—which had been her special job as far back as she could remember—she felt that, simply by behaving as always, she was keeping her entire family safe from some terrible danger. It made no sense; she knew, really, that she was not that important. Yet the feeling persisted and she deliberately sang as she worked.

When it was almost time to eat, Frieda was still out in the kitchen keeping an eye on things. Fritz, who had recently become addicted to western novels, was actually reading, of his own free will, the latest Zane Grey. Rudi came into the dining room and sat down, relaxing while he waited. Gretchen, coming down from upstairs, joined him and Anna.

"What are you giving Mama for her birthday?" she quizzed her older brother, sitting down across from him.

"I don't know yet," Rudi said. His face, half smiling a second before, grew unexpectedly grave. "I want it to be something really special this time."

Gretchen looked faintly surprised at his tone. "Last year was when she needed something special," she said, "when she turned forty."

"I suppose so," Rudi said, but his thoughtful expression did not change.

"Gretchen, come here for a minute," Frieda called. "I need you."

Gretchen departed.

"Anna, you think for me," Rudi said. "I need help too. I'm stuck."

She looked to see if he was teasing, but he wasn't.

"I want it to be a really happy present. Something happy that will last a long time."

Anna's feeling of danger returned instantly but she did not let him see it. Maybe she was wrong. As long as there was the slightest chance she might be mistaken, she would say nothing.

"There must be just the right thing," she said. "I promise I'll think."

Mama's birthday was not till April 29th. She still had lots of time.

That evening, she and Rudi worked on her algebra as usual. Then they read over some history together. Teaching her had been important, just as Papa had said, but in an unexpected way. Rudi had discovered in himself a love for teaching, and he had decided that when he graduated he would become a high school teacher.

"Soon there'll be nothing left for me to teach you," he said lightly as she looked for the page they wanted.

Anna glanced up quickly. "I'll always need help," she cried, as though he had said he was leaving her.

"Right now, I'm here," he said. "I don't think much of Cromwell, do you?"

"No," Anna said. "He's such a bully. But the king seems so idiotic that it's hard to know."

"It's always hard," her brother said.

Ten days later, Elisabeth Anna Schumacher was born. Her parents had simply turned Anna's name around and given it to their daughter.

"Because without you and your family helping things along, I don't think Franz would ever have had the courage to propose," Eileen Schumacher told them, when they went to see her and the baby. "And, in that case, there wouldn't have been an Elisabeth."

Anna was so pleased she was speechless, but Elisabeth Anna's mother seemed to understand. From that day onward, whenever Anna was not at home, at school, or at the library, she was sure to be at the Schumachers', helping to bring up her namesake.

But she did not forget Rudi's entreaty for help. In the middle of April, she decided what the gift for her mother should be.

"It's your turn to meet me after school," she said to Rudi. "I want to show you, not just tell you."

She took him straight to the pet shop. Leading the way, she went inside for the first time. There seemed to be puppies everywhere, standing on their hind paws, cuddled up together snoozing, tumbling over each other and growling in mock battles, or simply sitting and looking wistful. But Anna did not even look at the one that was her latest favorite, nor did she tell Rudi about the hours she had spent dreaming outside the shop window.

206

"A bird," she said, pointing. "A little yellow canary like the one we had in Frankfurt that she loved so. I just barely remember but I'm sure I'm right."

"Jenny," he said, his eyes as bright as hers. "She named it after Jenny Lind, the singer, although it wasn't a she at all. Only the males sing."

"That's right," the pet shop man said. "These are extra-special singers over here. Roller canaries. We've only had them a few days and I just have three left. It's funny. People seem to want a song in their homes these days. I guess it's not so funny at that."

"That's what I want," Rudi said. "Anna, you're a genius. A song in the house. How much are they?"

They were expensive. Rudi hesitated. Anna tugged at his sleeve.

"Let me pay half," she begged. "I have the money. I've been saving for a long time."

"Not for this. What for?" he asked.

The puppy Anna had been calling hers for the last month turned a perfect somersault and sat up, cocking his head on one side. She had called him McNair because he was a Scottie.

Now she did not even turn her head in his direction in case Rudi should guess.

"I changed my mind," she said. "I don't want what I thought I did any longer. I'm too grown-up. I'd honestly love to pay half for the bird."

"I shouldn't let you, but I've been saving too. I want

207

to give Papa some money before . . . Okay, Anna, it's a deal."

Anna wanted to ask, "Before what?" but the moment passed.

The shopkeeper promised to keep the bird for them till the birthday came.

When Mama saw the canary sitting fluffed up a bit, looking lonesome in his new cage, she was overcome. She hugged the pair of them, Rudi a little longer. That was only right, Anna thought. Rudi had always been her favorite and she had not tried to hide it, even though she had always denied it when they accused her outright.

"The man at the pet store said it might not sing for the first few days," Rudi warned, as Mama examined her new treasure.

Anna hoped the man at the store had been right and that the bird would sing then. The poor little thing looked so lost, so miserable.

"Pooh," said Mama. "What does some man at a store know about my bird?"

Then she made a soft trilling whistle that Anna remembered instantly, even though she had not heard it since Jenny died when she, Anna, was only six or seven.

The bird lifted his head, cocked it slightly, and listened intently.

The rest of the Soldens held their breaths.

Mama sang her coaxing little trill again.

And the bird sang back. Just a couple of notes but still singing.

"Where did you learn to do that, Mama?" Fritz asked, in awe.

"The birds taught me," Mama said proudly. "I used to go out into the woods in the summer and practice singing back to them when I was a child. And my mother always sang to her birds. What shall we call him?"

Nobody said anything for a moment. Then Anna said quickly, almost gruffly, "Why not call him Peter? That's a nice name."

"I never knew a bird called Peter," Mama said, studying the bird. "But I think maybe it suits him. Besides, I was in love once with a boy named Peter."

"You were?" "When?" "Who was he?" "I never heard of this." Questions came from all sides.

"He was my first love," Mama sighed, rolling her eyes dramatically. Then she laughed. "He lived next door to us when I was eight. But he moved away on my ninth birthday and I never heard of him again. I wanted to name Rudi 'Peter,' but your father did not think it such a good idea. It is all right for the bird though, Ernst, is it not?"

"Just right, if you like it," Papa said.

The bird suddenly sang again, four notes this time, without being invited to begin by Mama.

"It is settled. Peter he shall be," Mama said.

Anna smiled to herself. She could not have her puppy. But she had learned last week that Peter was Mr. McNair's first name.

209

19

FROM THE BEGINNING, nobody in the Solden household had been able to stay uninformed about the war. And, with April drawing to an end, more of Papa's predictions started to come true. Yet for Anna, April always remained the month she and Rudi bought Mama a bird for her birthday.

May was the month when the war moved from the radio, the movie newsreels, and the headlines in the newspaper, right into their home.

After he had written his examinations and helped celebrate Mama's birthday, Rudi waited only ten days before he enlisted. Later, looking back, Anna realized that he managed to spend time alone with each of them during that short interval.

He went to watch Fritz play basketball and they stayed up late talking. Anna, supposed to be asleep, listened to the rise and fall of their voices. It was easy to tell that Fritz was talking most.

He took Frieda on a bike hike. She almost didn't go, because something else came along that tempted her, and Anna was sick with envy for she would have loved to take Frieda's place, only she couldn't ride a bicycle because of her poor vision.

He sat, in the evenings and on weekends, watching Mama mending and ironing, encouraging her to tell him stories of the days when they had all been children.

Gretchen and he went to a band concert in the park. Anna asked if she might come too but Rudi said they probably wouldn't be back before her bedtime.

And he spent hours in the store with his father, helping enough so that Mama could take time off to do a thorough spring cleaning at home. There were often long gaps between customers, and the father and son spent them talking quietly or just sitting together.

Anna, growing more and more uneasy, turned up there, wanting to be with them. But after only ten minutes, Rudi told her to go home.

"Papa and I have things to discuss," he said, "but I'll meet you tomorrow after school and we'll go for a walk and have time by ourselves. You should be able to understand me needing to be alone with Papa. You've wanted him to yourself all your life."

She could not deny that. So she left.

He was there, waiting, when she came out of school.

"What did your dear friend Mr. McNair have to say today?" Rudi asked, his voice teasing.

Rudi was too smart. Anna blushed only a little.

"We didn't have math," she said.

Then they were in the park, the new grass under their feet, the sunlight falling on them through the thin screen of translucent new leaves.

"Anna," he said, "let's sit down on that bench over there. I have to . . . I want to talk to you. There's a thing I have to tell you."

"I don't want to hear," she said.

But she went to the bench.

And he told her that he was going to join the Navy the very next day.

She had no words to say. She sat, staring down at her hands gripped together in her lap.

"I wasn't going to tell anybody ahead of time but Papa," he went on, as though he had heard what was in her heart. "Yet Papa . . . well, Papa understands but he seems so tired. And I think our house will be a sad place for a while. Mama . . . she will not know how to bear it. The others are grown-up and away from her somehow, but you are the one she and Papa love most of all."

Anna looked up at him, blank astonishment taking the place of her misery for a moment.

"I know," he laughed. "When you were little, Mama thought you could do no right. But you have grown up so much, Anna. And you are kind. You see things the others don't notice. So I just wanted to ask you to help them all, especially Papa and Mama."

She help Papa? Mama maybe. Although that, too, seemed impossible. But Papa was the tower of strength on which she had always leaned. Papa helped her. Now things were different somehow, but she could not imagine herself helping Papa.

Rudi again seemed to read her thoughts. He reached out and took her hand.

"This war has hurt Papa more than any of us can guess," he said. "He does not talk of Aunt Tania but he thinks of her always. And he loves both Germany and England. And now he will be afraid for me."

"Then stay!" Anna cried, her voice choked and fierce. "He has enough trouble. I can't help. You mustn't go."

He replaced her hand carefully in her lap and stood up.

"I have to," he said simply. "I know it will hurt him. But I have to. I can't explain it so you will understand. . . . Anna, do you remember Herr Keppler?"

For a moment, she had no idea what he was talking about. Then she did remember. Herr Keppler had been the new headmaster in their school just before they had left Germany. He was a Nazi. He had been a cruel man, and once he had not let them sing a song, a song about freedom. How they feared him! How helpless he made

213

them feel! She remembered something else too, something she had remembered when the letter about Aunt Tania's arrest came: Gerda Hoffman, a girl in her class, whose father had just disappeared one night while his family was waiting for him to come home to supper— Gerda with her wounded eyes who had also vanished but who had appeared in Anna's dreams for months.

"Yes, I remember," she said.

"Well, that's why I'm going," he said. "So the people like Herr Keppler won't win. And so someone will help all the Aunt Tanias. Say you'll help, Anna. Say you'll do everything you can. Promise me."

She was crying now and she did not even try to stop. But she nodded her head and then stood up as tall as she could beside him.

"Have my handkerchief," he said.

She blew her nose loudly. It was such a familiar, ordinary sound that it cheered both of them. She wiped away the tears and did not let others fall.

"Why are you going in the Navy?" she asked, keeping her voice as steady as she could. "Paula's cousin went in the Army."

"Well, maybe I'm a bit mixed up about it all still," Rudi said. "But I don't want to have to fight inside Germany ever and I don't want to have to drop bombs on Frankfurt. There are other people there besides Herr Keppler. He's probably off somewhere in a uniform."

"I don't think so," Anna said. "He bullied children. I don't think he was truly brave."

She did not know how she managed to eat supper without anyone asking her what was wrong. Papa looked at her but he knew. Watching Rudi making jokes, complimenting Gretchen on the cabbage rolls, getting the whole family to laugh, stiffened her spine. She passed her plate for more apple dumpling.

But the next morning, after Rudi left, Mama collapsed. On Sunday she stayed in bed, refusing to attend church with the rest. She had always been the person who saw to it that nobody ever missed a church service, unless he or she were seriously ill, so it seemed strange and wrong to be sitting in their usual pew without her. When Gretchen went to call her for lunch, Mama kept her back turned and said she had already eaten.

"But she can't have," Gretchen said. "Nothing's gone."

"She must be ill," Papa said. "I'll go and talk to her."

When Papa came out of the bedroom, he looked more anxious than before.

"She says she's not sick," he reported, "but she won't talk to me except to tell me not to call the doctor. She is missing Rudi, of course, but lying in there alone is so unlike her. I don't know how to reach her."

Anna heard the words and knew that both her parents needed help. But what could she do? Nothing, whatever Rudi might think. She went up to her own bed and sought escape in a new book she had got out of the library. It was called *How Green Was My Valley* and was written by Richard Llewellyn. She loved the poetry of it and the people, but today even Huw Morgan's magic

215

storytelling could not free her from worrying about Mama and missing Rudi.

The next morning, Mama got up and went to work as usual and everyone felt relieved. She continued to eat little and remained mostly silent, but nobody felt much like talking anyway. At least she was back with them.

That was the day Germany invaded Holland.

Anna watched Mama pushing food around on her plate that night. Then, before anyone could break the leaden atmosphere, Klara Solden left the table, went into her bedroom, and closed the door. They all sat mesmerized, staring at the door shut in their faces.

"She hardly spoke to me today," Papa said. "She waited on people but said as little as possible. She must be sick with grief. I'll take her something later."

They got through the meal somehow. Anna had homework to do. She kept busy till bedtime. But that night in bed, she began to wonder about her mother. Was Mama really so stricken? It was silly. Rudi had not even left Toronto yet. He was on a naval training ship in Lake Ontario, and before long he would be able to come home on leave. She knew how Mama must feel. Rudi was Mama's firstborn and favorite child. Still, could it be that Mama just did not know how to stop acting tragic? Anna could remember times when she herself had sworn positively never to speak to Mama again or made some other rash vow. How soon she had wanted to break her own word and yet how difficult it had been to stop posing as angry or injured.

Mama wouldn't act that way though. She was not a child.

Still, Anna wondered. And the next night, when Mama would not come to the table, Anna got up in sudden anger, filled a plate with food, put it and cutlery and a glass of water on a tray, and headed for that shut door.

"She won't eat it, Anna," Gretchen said, looking wretched with worry.

"Oh, yes, she will," said Anna. And setting her jaw exactly as she used to do when she was nine years old and about to defy her mother, she marched into Mama's room, Fritz jumping up to open the door.

"Sit up, Mama," she said, in a voice totally lacking in sympathy. "You're going to eat your supper."

"Take it away," Mama moaned. "Leave me alone."

"You ought to be ashamed," Anna said. "Papa is getting pale with worry over you. Gretchen can't eat. Rudi hasn't had any letters from anybody because we are so anxious about you. He's probably getting thin too, and all you can do is lie there and feel sorry for yourself." She gulped in a deep breath and rushed on while her mood held. "I know it was hard when he first left, but that's over and everybody but you is trying to keep going. I think you're just sulking by now and can't stop—but you can EAT, so sit up!"

Her mother turned over and stared up at the youngest of her children.

"Enough of that talk, Miss Anna Elisabeth Solden," Mama snapped, her indignation a match for Anna's. "No-

217

body is going to starve around here as long as I have a word to say. What is your Papa thinking of?"

"You," Anna said, turning, the tray still in her hands. "I'll go tell Gretchen to set another place."

"You set it," Mama called after her. "Setting the table is your job."

The others sat like sheep, staring, as Anna plunked the tray down on the sideboard and set her mother's place with much banging of cutlery.

"Wake up," she said to them all. "Mama's coming out here. Try to look alive."

Papa burst out laughing.

"Bravo, Anna," he said. "I thought that temper vanished years ago."

"Not when I need it," Anna said.

But suddenly she felt her knees wobble.

Then a familiar voice spoke from behind her, not the sad voice they had heard since Saturday, but Klara Solden's brisk, sensible one.

"Set that child down on a chair, Ernst, before she falls over," she said. "It's not every day she gives her mother a good scolding. When you said I was sulking," she went on, looking at Anna, "all at once, I knew you were right. Me, sulking! At my time of life. I can't think where you ever learned to give a tongue-lashing like that."

She gave Anna a suspicious look.

Anna gave back a demure smile.

"From Papa, I think," she said.

The family, freed from tension, roared with laughter. Mama herself joined in. Papa had never scolded any of them, that they could remember, and she knew it as well as Anna.

"Well," she said, recovering, "now let us praise God, Ernst, that we are together and . . ." Her voice faltered. ". . . and ask his blessing on Rudi, wherever he is, and eat our supper, as Anna has ordered."

Anna, sitting next to Papa, felt strength coming back. She had wondered if she would ever smile again. Now she grinned at her mother.

"He's right here in Toronto on the H.M.C.S. *York*," she said. "Probably bored to death."

"I hope he sends a picture soon of him in his uniform," Frieda said, "so I can show it off at school."

Mama sighed. Then she patted Frieda's hand.

"I always liked men in uniform myself, didn't I, Ernst," she said.

Papa, smiling at his wife, nodded and then looked down at his youngest daughter so lovingly that she had all the reward she needed.

I am trying, Rudi, she thought, and pulled her chair closer to the table so she could eat.

20

KNOWING RUDI WAS SO CLOSE by made Anna almost
forget that he would be leaving for Halifax in six weeks.
She missed him most when it came time to study. She
had not realized how many difficulties she had grown
accustomed to taking to him.

At the end of the first week, she took the pages he had
worked on with her, with the big black numbers he had
made, and went to Mr. McNair.

"I was sorry to hear that Rudi had left school," he said.
"It is true then?"

"He's in the Navy," Anna said. "But he waited till he
had finished his examinations before he went."

"He'll do well, that boy," Mr. McNair said. "Now what is all this you've brought to show me?"

When he looked at the pages, they explained themselves. But what would he do about them? Anna waited, tense, knowing how busy he was.

"Come in right after four," he said, handing her back the pages in a matter-of-fact way. "I don't promise to be as good a tutor as your brother but we'll see how we get along. Just remember, Anna, tell me when I go too fast or when you can't see something."

She promised she would and hurried from the room.

When she got home, she went straight to the bird cage and said to the bird, "Beautiful, wonderful, perfect Peter! You're the best Peter in the world."

Gretchen looked at her in surprise as the little canary sang happily, pleased with the attention.

"I didn't know you liked him all that much," Gretchen said. "Not that he isn't a nice bird . . . but wonderful? Perfect?"

"Peter understands," Anna replied, grinning at her sister's puzzled expression. "It's just between him and me. He's very understanding, aren't you, Peter?"

"Since you're in such a marvelous mood," returned Gretchen, "how about dusting the downstairs?"

After three weeks, Rudi had a leave. He had to be back at the training ship by nine o'clock, so it seemed as though he was just there and gone. Still it was wonderful seeing him. He really and truly looked like a sailor. Anna had

221

not believed he actually would, but there he was with his big middy collar, his bell-bottom trousers, his tie—"tied just so, I'm telling you!"—and a ribbon around his sailor hat. Mama was so busy gloating over him and feeding him and running to touch him and getting hugged by him that she did not cry till he had gone.

In May, Germany occupied the Netherlands. In June, France was defeated. Britain seemed terribly small, set so close to Europe, but the words of Winston Churchill, Britain's new Prime Minister, sounded throughout the Empire like a rallying cry. The Soldens heard them through Papa's radio:

"We shall go on to the end, we shall fight in France, we shall fight on the seas and oceans, we shall fight with growing confidence and growing strength in the air, we shall defend our Island, whatever the cost may be, we shall fight on the beaches, we shall fight on the landing grounds, we shall fight in the fields and in the streets, we shall fight in the hills; we shall never surrender. . . ."

Just before school ended, Maggie's father, too, joined the Navy. "As soon as they attacked Holland, he told Mother he had to go," Maggie reported. She and Anna were drawn closer than ever.

Since Mr. Lloyd had typed her Easter exams in big type too, Anna was not surprised when her finals arrived in the same way on her desk. But she was startled when he called her out of line, halfway through the week, to tell her that he had marked her paper the night before and that she had received 82 in geography. His kindness to her, while never obvious to others, had remained constant and she beamed at him, even getting a small smile in return.

She was troubled about it that night, however. His persecution of other students with German backgrounds, though lower-keyed than on that first terrifying morning, continued. The rumor was that he had a twin brother who was killed fighting against Germans the day before the 1918 armistice was signed. She guessed Mr. Lloyd himself would not have been able to fight in that war because of his poor vision. So she understood a little how he must have suffered. But that was no reason for turning his hatred against students who had not even been born when his brother died. He was nice to her now. Why couldn't he see that the others were all right too?

Some customers who had stopped shopping at Papa's store had come back when they learned Rudi was in the Navy. But her father had been the same man before Rudi enlisted, a man who so opposed dictatorship that he had emigrated from his homeland to seek freedom for his family. Dr. Schumacher was suffering from persecution too, she was sure.

She could not face up to all the people, most of them strangers, who automatically classed all Germans as Nazi sympathizers. But she could speak to one man and try to make him see. At least, she hoped she could.

The next afternoon, she told the others to go on home without her, saying only that she had something she wanted to do at the school. She stayed occasionally to talk with Miss Sutcliff about some poem she had discovered and she let the gang conclude that she was doing it once again. Maggie looked skeptical but left without asking any pressing questions.

Mr. Lloyd was sitting at his desk with a stack of examination papers in front of him. Anna realized how difficult it must be for him to read all that scrawly handwriting. She almost turned back. Instead, she walked forward and sat down in her usual front seat, facing him. It would be easier to talk if she did not have to stand.

"Yes, Miss Solden?" he said.

She began badly and saw, before she had reached the end of her second labored sentence, that he was already deeply angry.

"Mr. Lloyd, please," she said, desperately, abandoning her prepared speech. "I know I sound rude and you want me to go but I have to tell somebody. I have to. So, please, listen."

He was silent but his eyes stayed cold.

Then she plunged in, saying things all out of order, and told him far more than she had intended. She poured out the story of Aunt Tania, of Gerda Hoffman, even of Herr Keppler.

"You would have been right to hate Herr Keppler," she finished, positive she had wasted her time and that he had not understood a word she had said. "But don't you see that Carl and Paula and Fred Weber would all hate him too? I know that you didn't like my brother Rudi but he's nicer and anyway, he's in the Navy now." She swallowed hard and made herself go on to the end. "Someday he might even be killed, fighting against . . . against tyranny, just as your brother was."

"Be silent," Mr. Lloyd barked.

She sat where she was, not speaking but unable to get up and leave the room at once because she was shaking so. The teacher drew a deep breath. Then he said, "I said before that you have courage. I understand what you have been saying. I have been bitter for so long I doubt that I can change. But I apologize for all that I have done that made it necessary for you to come and say these things to me. I think you had better go now, Miss Solden."

"Yes, sir," she said.

She managed to stand up and get as far as the door. She almost missed his parting words.

"Give my regards to your brother when you see him next."

"Yes, sir," she said again and left.

She felt limp. She understood better Rudi's need to go to war. She had gone to battle. She was not sure whether she had won a decisive victory but she was glad she had seen it through. Even after she reached home, however, she felt shaken.

Mr. Churchill should have put in, "We shall fight in the schools," she thought that night before she slept.

When she got her report card, she was delighted to find that she had not failed in a single subject. She had barely passed in P.T. and home economics but she topped the class in English and came in fifth in algebra. Much to her secret satisfaction, she beat Suzy by four marks.

Papa went to the school to thank Mr. McNair and the others for the special help they had given her. When he returned, he gave Anna a long thoughtful look.

"What is it? What did they say?" Anna demanded, unnerved by his gaze.

The rest of the family laughed at her. Mama, as anxious as Anna, waited.

"It seems Rudi isn't the only genius in this house, Klara," he said. "Both Mr. McNair and Miss Sutcliff insist that Anna should go to university. They just couldn't agree on which course she should take."

"Whatever would Frau Schmidt say?" Mama exclaimed. Frau Schmidt had been Anna's first teacher long ago in Frankfurt and had told the Soldens that Anna was impossible to teach.

"That Mr. Lloyd you have all complained about so much seemed a very good man to me," Papa went on, looking around at his assembled children. "He too thinks you have promise, Anna. We'll have to see what we can do, when the time comes."

The others objected loudly to Mr. Lloyd being praised. Anna said nothing but her spirits soared. She had been right in having faith in Mr. Lloyd.

I guess that was what Mr. Appleby meant, she mused. Something like it anyway.

Then Rudi was shipped to Halifax. He came to say good-bye. This time, it was harder to laugh. Halifax seemed far away. Anna just barely remembered landing there when the ship brought them from Germany. It had been a cold gray place, she thought, or was that the way she first saw Toronto? Rudi, however, refused to let them sit and stare solemnly at him. He had a host of stories. All the injections he had to have! All the floors he had scrubbed! The whole art of folding a sailor collar, he explained to them, and how glad he had been that Mama had made him learn to make his bed.

"Some of the guys never made a bed before!" he said.

"You didn't make yours all that often," Gretchen said. "Just pulled it up and that was it. How many hundred times have we done his bed, Frieda?"

"Thousands is more like it," Frieda said.

Papa told him what the teachers had said about Anna. Rudi looked at her with a pleased, almost smug, look on his face.

"I've known that for quite a while, Papa," he said. "But she needs discipline. Keep after her for me while I'm gone. Mr. McNair will help, I'm sure."

Only Papa was going to the station. They crowded around Rudi, hugging and kissing him. Rudi leaned

227

down to Anna and whispered in her ear, "Keep it up. I'm counting on you."

She nodded, clutching at his arm, not wanting to let him go.

"And listen for the singing, Anna," he said suddenly, with a last grin, "whatever happens."

It was his private message for her, telling her he remembered all they had talked about.

"I will," she called after him. "I promise."

It was a full and happy summer. Then, in August, on a hot sunny afternoon, when Anna was standing out in front of the house, finishing off an ice cream cone, the telegram came.

She was curious. She followed the boy as he left his bike and went to the door. Curious but not afraid. Rudi was safe enough on the H.M.C.S. *Cornwallis*. He had not had his embarkation leave yet.

Gretchen signed for the wire and then hesitated. It was addressed to Papa.

"I'll take it over to the store," Anna offered.

It was a dull afternoon. For once, nobody had been free to do anything and the library was closed. The telegram promised some excitement. She did feel a stir of apprehension. Something could have happened. As she half hurried along the hot sidewalk, she thought of Aunt Tania. But she dismissed the thought almost immediately. It had been such a long time without word.

Yet suppose it were. Just suppose . . . She broke into a run. It must be something! People don't send telegrams for nothing. And if Aunt Tania had escaped, wouldn't that be what she would do, send word the fastest way?

She burst into the store.

"A telegram, Papa," she cried.

Papa, no expectation in his face, came forward and took the envelope from her outstretched hand. Anna opened her mouth to tell them her idea of what it might say. Then she looked down at the yellow paper as Papa unfolded it. She waited for him to tell.

He was silent for what seemed forever.

Then he scrunched the paper up and put it into his pocket. He turned to his wife, ignoring the people in the store and Anna too.

"It is Rudi," he said. "There has been an accident. He is in a hospital in Halifax."

"What's wrong?" Mama almost screamed, although her voice was not really so loud; it was just so filled with fear. "Do they say what is wrong?"

"Klara . . ." Papa began. He took his glasses off, polished them, and put them back on. "Klara," he repeated as though he did not know any other words.

"Ernst, tell me!"

Anna had never heard Mama speak in that voice before. It snapped like a whip. Her father's head jerked up. He faced his wife across half the store. When he answered, he spoke clearly, but also in a voice Anna had not before heard, a voice she would hear in her memory all her life.

"They say he is blind."

229

21

PAPA DID NOT GO to get Rudi until September was half over. Dr. Schumacher made many telephone calls the night the telegram came. Finally, he got in touch with the doctor in charge of Rudi's case. Afterward he and Papa came immediately home.

"Dr. Bricker says Rudi is doing well and seems quite cheerful," he said, "but he is not ready to travel yet and he has said that he does not want any of the family to come. He also told me that Rudi is suffering from profound shock but is being very courageous. He sounded very impressed by him."

"How did it happen?" Mama asked. "Did he say how

230

long it would be before he is better? He will get better, won't he?"

"He said it was some freak accident. Cleaning fluid got splashed into his face. Both eyes were badly burned. When the burns heal, there will be scars. He holds out no hope that Rudi will be able to see again. I'm so sorry, Klara."

"Cleaning fluid," Mama repeated. "But how . . . ?"

"It was no one's fault, Dr. Bricker said. He didn't give me the details. How it happened doesn't lessen the tragedy."

Anna heard the words but could not make herself feel they were true. Not about Rudi with his eyes that were bluer than anyone's. She waited dully for Mama to begin to cry. Mama sat very straight and did not shed a tear.

She doesn't believe it either, Anna thought.

Later, lying in bed unable to sleep, she suddenly remembered thinking one day that it would be simpler for her if she were blind. Then she had seen something. What? The sunlight turning Maggie's hair to gold. And she had known what a miracle vision was. Then she thought of Rudi and wept.

But the days that followed were busy ones and she had little time to brood. She set out for school on the first morning of the new term with scarcely a qualm. She would have to explain about her poor eyesight to any new teachers but she was getting used to explaining. She had come to understand and deal with her own limitations in a new way during the previous year. She had even discovered hitherto hidden abilities. She could serve a volleyball perfectly!

It had been arranged ahead of time that she and Maggie would not be separated. The two of them had gone to see Mr. Appleby about it before school ended. After confronting Mr. Lloyd, Anna no longer found those secretaries formidable.

As it turned out, the whole gang was put into the same class with Miss Sutcliff as their homeroom teacher. This fall, Anna, instead of going on home as she had the year before because she could not see, went with the others to the school football games. She loved wearing the school colors, long white and green ribbons streaming down from a small rosette pinned to her coat. She knew all the cheers. Any friend of Suzy's could not help learning them. Suzy chanted them whenever there was a moment's silence. Anna found herself having a wonderful time, even though she had no clear idea of what was happening in the game. She groaned, screamed, and jumped up and down with everyone else. Maggie tried to remember to tell her afterward what they had been excited about.

She felt guilty having fun when she thought of Rudi. Yet she knew that sitting alone and sorrowing over his tragedy would help neither him nor her. Mama, this time, did nothing dramatic like refusing to eat. She too realized that the only way to hold on to her sanity and help her family through this dark time was to behave as normally as possible. Anna understood her mother better than ever before.

A letter arrived before Rudi came home. He had dictated it to someone. It sent everyone individual greetings. The others looked relieved because his words sounded so normal. But Anna heard the words meant for her without any response except uneasiness. "Hi, Anna. Keep smiling." He had never told her to keep smiling before. Why hadn't he said something with meaning?

He asked only one thing, that they somehow manage to give him a room to himself.

"I know this will make a problem," he said, "but if Anna could move in with the other girls, I'd be glad to have her corner."

They moved Fritz down to the couch in the living room instead. He didn't care. Anna sighed with relief and she was sure her two sisters did too. There just was not room for the three of them, each so different, in that one bedroom. Gretchen and Frieda had over the years worked out an arrangement by which they managed to keep the peace, but with Anna added it would never have worked.

Then Papa went to get Rudi. The house seemed extra quiet, waiting. Mama baked Rudi's favorite cookies. Nobody talked about it much. Nobody knew what to say. But everyone was nervous.

Before they felt ready, the two were home, Papa, looking older than Anna had ever seen him, and Rudi with dark glasses on and a cane in his hand, smiling, saying the right things.

"He's so normal," Gretchen half whispered when Papa had taken him up the stairs, away from them, "but . . ."

But he wasn't normal at all, Anna thought, not saying the words aloud. And it's not just that he's blind. He's gone away from us inside. His feelings are blind too.

In the following week, a routine was set up. Rudi ate alone in his room. He came downstairs in the evenings when the whole family was home, and sat in the living room with them. He listened to the news with Papa. He told Mama how good her torte was. He insisted that she not stay at home with him, that he just wanted to rest by himself. He never mentioned his blindness. When he needed help, he asked for it directly, in as few words as possible. It was only then that the studied cheer went out of his voice and they could hear the hurt.

"But what can we *do*?" Frieda said desperately one evening, when Rudi had already gone up to his room.

"Give him time," Papa said tiredly. "That's what Dr. Bricker told me. He said he is wounded in spirit as well as in his eyes. Just leave him to get over it, he said."

"He won't let us do anything else," Mama said. Now tears did come. "Yet he does seem cheerful. He eats well. I think . . . I'm sure he is getting better."

Anna knew he was not. She could hear him in the night when he thought everyone was sleeping. Often he

234

paced back and forth, back and forth in his room, with no light on. Anna knew he did not need light but still it made it all the more terrible somehow. Then she heard him crying. She knew how he must look. She had seen him the day the news came about Aunt Tania. She had reached out to him then. Maybe now she could do it again.

She lay still, listening.

What could she say?

He did not know anyone heard him. He never let them see him cry.

She stayed where she was.

The next afternoon, she went up to him and asked him about a problem she was having with geometry.

"I can't help you, Anna," he said, quite calmly. "Ask Mr. McNair."

"But, Rudi," she started, forcing herself to go on in spite of his indifference, "if you could just explain . . ."

"I'm sorry. I can't," he said. "You're too clever for me now, Anna."

She retreated and sat by herself, thinking hard.

The girls at school were fascinated by Rudi. To them, he seemed a wounded war hero. In a way he was, Anna knew. But she did not want to talk about him.

Finally a night came when she could no longer lie still and listen. She got up and went to his door.

"Rudi," she said softly, to the pacing in the darkness. "Rudi, can I do anything for you?"

There was a silence in the room, a silence so complete it was frightening. She waited.

Then a rasping voice said, "Leave me alone, Anna. I'm sorry I wakened you."

She stood still, not sure what to do.

"Please," he said, his voice a whisper now, "just leave me alone."

She turned and was halfway out the door when he asked abruptly, "Have I ever wakened you before?"

Anna swallowed. She must make him believe her.

"No," she said steadily, "I just happened to wake up."

"Good night," he said.

"Good night," she returned, yawning what she hoped sounded like a normal, sleepy yawn.

She had not talked with Rudi; she had talked to a stranger. When she reached her bed, she had to bury her face in the pillow or he would have heard her cry.

The next afternoon, after school, she went to Mrs. Schumacher. She phoned first from the office at school. She let the secretary assume she was phoning her parents. Although nobody seemed to be listening, she kept her voice low.

Mrs. Schumacher did not ask her to speak more clearly. She simply said, "Of course, you may come. As soon as you can get here is fine."

As Anna neared the Schumachers' house, she felt apprehensive. What if she could not make Mrs. Schumacher understand? Yet she was the most understanding person, except for Papa, whom Anna knew. She had, after all, understood Anna herself when nobody else could get past the sullen, stubborn, uncaring face she had turned toward the world, the wall of pride she had built around herself. Now, she was sure Rudi was behind a wall, too. And Anna longed to find a way to get him out.

Mrs. Schumacher opened the door before Anna had time to ring the bell.

"Elisabeth's sleeping," she said. "She's a very considerate child really. She won't wake up for a couple of hours."

Anna smiled. She had spent a lot of time with Elisabeth that summer. Mrs. Schumacher had taught her how to give the baby a bath, had let her feed her and take her out in the carriage. Anna had loved pushing that buggy along, pretending the baby inside it was hers, sometimes. She was proud to be trusted with Elisabeth. But right now she was glad the baby was out of the way.

Mrs. Schumacher led the way into the living room. She seemed to know, from the beginning, that this was not one of Anna's customary visits, that she had come about something serious. She knew, of course, about Rudi. But not about his nights. Only Anna knew that.

Anna told Eileen Schumacher everything, all the small things and the big ones that were worrying her.

A man from the Canadian National Institute for the Blind had come to see Rudi, soon after Papa brought him home. Anna had just come in from school so she stayed to listen.

"Rudi was perfectly polite," she told Mrs. Schumacher.

"But, at the end, he said, 'I don't think I'm quite ready yet for the things you're suggesting, sir. I just want to rest at the moment. I'll have my father telephone your office when I think you can help me.' "

"That sounds good," Mrs. Schumacher said. "It sounds as though he realizes he has to give himself a while to adjust, and then he'll ask for help."

"It does sound like that," agreed Anna, struggling to put her anxiety into words. "His words always sound all right. But there's nothing underneath what he says. It's as though he's not really there. Just politeness and words but not Rudi himself. I'm sure he only listens enough so he can make the right answers. Otherwise he doesn't care. And nothing he says really means anything."

She paused and took a deep breath. Mrs. Schumacher waited for her to go on.

"And, oh, in the night . . ." Anna's story came spilling out.

"Once I heard him praying to die," Anna said, the horror of that moment still dark in her eyes. "He begged! But that's not the most frightening thing. It's hard for me to know how to say it. To me, the worst part is that he is going further and further away from us. He's disappearing, escaping maybe, into some safe secret place where nobody can reach him or hurt him anymore."

She stopped, trying to get her thoughts in order. Although she didn't want to repeat herself, she had to make it clear. Her friend still said nothing, seeing Anna had not finished.

"What's wrong is you can't live in that place. I've been somewhere like it. A little like it, anyway. It's like being shut up inside a shell with no way out. I remember. I still dream about it sometimes."

"Oh, Anna," Eileen Schumacher said.

Anna paid no attention. She was not sorry for that little girl now; she was worried about Rudi.

"When I was small and everything seemed so hard and Rudi was mean, I went there, but I couldn't love anybody from inside that place. You and Bernard and Ben and Isobel and Papa all rescued me. You just broke the shell, a little at a time, until you could come in and I couldn't stop you. You could come in and I could come out."

Mrs. Schumacher smiled at that. She even laughed softly.

"You were extremely prickly at first, I must admit," she said. "I thought of you, I remember, as a little porcupine with all its quills sticking out. And I can see why you are concerned now. But what do you want to do?"

"I want to rescue Rudi," Anna said simply. "I think— I don't know why—that we could wait too long. He might go so far in we'd never be able to bring him back."

Mrs. Schumacher sat still, on a low hassock, her arms clasped around her knees. She looked at the child—no, the young woman—facing her.

"I think you have a plan, don't you, Anna?" she said. "I can see it in your face. Tell me. That's what you really came for, isn't it?"

Anna nodded, not surprised that Mrs. Schumacher had

239

guessed. She had always been good at reading the minds of the children she taught. But she wanted this plan to be a secret. It had to be or it wouldn't work. This was going to be the tricky part. She had no choice but to trust her old teacher.

"It's like this," she said, and explained. She did not confide her whole idea, not the last part she would play in it by herself, if she had to. She would do it only if the first part wasn't enough, and whatever happened, it would be between Rudi and her, no one else.

"Can you help?" Anna asked. "Will you?"

"That's a tall order, Anna, but I think perhaps I can. I can try anyway," Mrs. Schumacher said slowly, thinking ahead as she spoke. "I'll have to do some persuading but Franz can help. You don't mind him knowing, Anna?"

Anna shook her head. She felt giddy with relief. There had been the chance that Mrs. Schumacher would not go along with the idea.

"Maybe, very likely in fact, we're going about this all wrong and we should leave it to the professionals," Mrs. Schumacher said, hesitating for one moment.

"I know Rudi better than anyone," Anna said, surprised to realize this was true. "I know how he can put people off. I think . . . you see, he was so mean to me once, not just one time but often, back a few years before I knew you even. We don't speak of it now but he feels sorry when he thinks of it. Or he did, before he went away. Then last year we got to be a sort of team. Maybe, because of those things, I can get through to him. I do want to try. If I fail and it doesn't help, then someone else, some grown-up, can still do the professional things."

Getting ready to put Anna's plan into operation took nearly a month. She had to go over to the Schumachers' almost every day after school.

"What's gotten into you? I've hardly seen you for days," Maggie protested.

"It's something I'm trying to do for Rudi," Anna said, knowing that would silence all objections.

"Can we help?" Suzy wanted to know.

Anna shook her head.

"I can't talk about it so don't ask," she said.

Can *I* help? she wondered.

It was too late to back down. The night came when she had to try it, good or bad, right or wrong. She went up to Rudi's room and got things ready in an out-of-the-way corner where he would be sure not to trip over anything. She went back down, waited the long, long hours till bedtime, and tried not to grow so afraid, while she was waiting, that she would be unable, in the end, to carry her plan through. She also had to keep all of this inner turmoil hidden from her family. She had never in her life been more grateful than she was that night when Mama said, as usual:

"Off to bed, Anna. Sleep well."

The time had almost come.

241

22

ANNA HAD WORRIED ABOUT FALLING asleep but she was far too tied up in knots even to doze. She heard all the noises of the household settling down: water running in the bathroom, Papa and Mama talking downstairs, light switches being clicked off, the last news broadcast signing off with "God Save the King," beds creaking. Papa began to snore. After an endless stretch of time, she heard Rudi start to walk, back and forth, as though he were locked in a cage.

She took a small flashlight, borrowed from Dr. Schumacher, eased out of bed without making a sound, inched her way cautiously to his bedroom, opened the door soundlessly and slid her body around it, beamed the thin line of light down at the talking book machine and reached for the knob that turned it on. She waited till Rudi was on the far side of the room. He was talking to himself. She couldn't hear the words, only muttering, but they made him miss the one little click. She had worried about that click ahead of time and never dreamed it would be so simple.

Breathing shallowly, doing her level best to keep her hand steady, she moved the phonograph needle into place.

"*A Tale of Two Cities,*" a man's voice read out, startling even Anna, who had known what was coming, "by Charles Dickens. Read by Stanley Wellman."

Having practiced at the Schumachers' over and over, Anna then moved the needle a little farther on in order to miss all the part about it being a talking book to be used exclusively by blind people, and to reach the story itself. It caught the tail end of the last word of what she wanted to skip and then went on, the deep voice speaking the words with love, with respect, exactly the way they should be read.

"It was the worst of times, it was the best of times, it was the age of wisdom, it was the age of foolishness, it was the epoch of belief. . . ."

"What is it? Turn it off. Stop it! Who's there?" Rudi cried out.

243

She had been amazed he had let the record play that long. She switched it off.

"It's only me, Anna," she said. "That was the first record of a talking book. I picked it because I knew you liked it, even though you had read it before. I thought . . ."

"Anna, please, I told you, leave me alone," Rudi said.

"I will in a minute," she answered, keeping on even though she could hear her voice starting to shake. "But first I have to do one more thing. Listen, just this once. I want to read you something."

Rudi said nothing but she could feel his mind set against her. If anything, the wall was stronger.

Slowly, painstakingly slowly, she began to read. She had marked off the breaks in the first paragraph with bits of paper glued to the page. Since she had been following, she knew how to pick up exactly where the reader on the record had been cut off.

"It . . . was . . . the . . . epoch . . . of . . . in . . . cre . . . du . . . li . . . ty . . . it . . . was . . . the . . . sea . . . son . . . of . . . light. . . ."

"Anna." He stopped her.

"Yes?" she said.

"Why are you reading like that, so slowly?"

"It's very fast for me. I only know the basic alphabet, none of the abbreviations. If I didn't have it practically memorized, I'd have been slower still," she said, not giving him a direct answer, trying to make him go on talking.

"Anna," he said again.

"Yes?" Anna said, her heart lifting a fraction for his voice sounded alive. Not warm or understanding or welcoming. But curious and really Rudi's.

"How are you reading?"

"In Braille," Anna said.

"Were you looking at it?"

"No. How could I be? I didn't turn on the light."

There was a long silence. Then she began to talk to him in a quiet, level, almost angry voice.

"Rudi, stop being the way you are. You're not you at all. If I can read Braille after only a few lessons from Mrs. Schumacher, you can too. You can listen to this book all night here in the darkness instead of pacing up and down, up and down."

"So you did hear me other nights," he said softly, bitterly.

"Yes. I've always heard you. But I'm talking about something else. You're going away inside. Mama says you're getting better. You have even Papa nearly fooled. . . ."

"But not smart little Anna," he mocked.

"No, not me," she said. "Because I know how it is."

"You know!" he jeered again.

But once more she was glad, for he sounded ready to fight. She had not heard him ready to fight for weeks. Now she would have to use her last weapon, the one she had withheld until now.

"I couldn't see much till I was nine," she said, "and you, you called me Awkward Anna and made fun of me and kept saying I was stupid. Do you remember that? I was more afraid of you than of anyone."

"But I didn't know," he said, taken off guard by her sudden attack.

"Oh, it's all over long ago, that hurting. And I wasn't like you because I didn't know either that I couldn't see properly. I believed you were right, that I was stupid and clumsy and no good. I believed you so much that I went away inside myself where you couldn't reach me to keep hurting. Like you, now."

"Where's the phonograph?" he asked suddenly.

Anna knew when to stop.

"Let me turn on the light for myself," she said, "and I can get you to it. I used a tiny flashlight to help me find it before, so you wouldn't hear me and I could surprise you."

"You're just lucky I didn't have a heart attack," her brother said, as she pulled his hand into the crook of her elbow and led him to the talking book machine. Showing him how to operate it was simple. "The records go around much more slowly than on our own phonograph," she explained, "and here are all the other records that make up the rest of the book."

He picked them up and carefully put them back down.

"I can teach you the Braille alphabet, which is how everybody begins, after school—if you help me with my math, that is."

She held her breath while she waited. Had she gone too far?

Then he laughed, a cracked little laugh that sounded something like a sob. But Anna knew it was laughter.

"Go back to bed, Little Stupid, little Awkward Anna," he said. "We'll see what tomorrow brings when we get there. Turn out the light when you go."

She got up and left him, without another word, because she couldn't speak with such a lump in her throat. She ran to her alcove, fell onto her bed and lay there, listening.

Would the pacing begin again?

What had she done?

He hadn't promised anything.

"It was the best of times, it was the worst of times . . ." the voice began again.

Then it said, *". . . it was the season of light, it was the season of darkness, it was the spring of hope. . . ."*

Anna hugged her pillow to her and let the tears of joy come any old way they wanted to.

23

THE TWO OF THEM KEPT their secret for a week. It wasn't that hard. Anna simply disappeared up the stairs when she came home from school, as though she were busy reading before it was time to help with supper. She was extremely careful not to get a detention, even to the point of not answering when her friends whispered things to her. She tried to explain without really telling them anything. She hoped they forgave her. She was sure that Maggie at least would. But she was too excited at the moment to care if they didn't. The other three Solden young people were busy with extracurricular activities at school and were always late coming home. Mama and Papa, of course, were at the store.

Later, when Rudi stopped minding, everyone would know the story, or most of it. Some parts would always stay just between Anna and her brother.

The first afternoon, when she ran up to his room, she was terribly afraid she would find him withdrawn again and angry at her too. But the moment she arrived, he deluged her with talk.

"I'm half asleep because I stayed up all night listening to that book," he told her, "but I'm awake now, Anna, and I'm here, back from wherever you said I'd gone. I still don't see any future but I can see a right now."

"The present moment is all you ever really have," Anna said, sounding wise. Then she had to laugh and admit she was only quoting something she had heard their father say once.

"It was partly that . . . oh, I couldn't bear to start back at the beginning and ask some stranger, 'Is this A?' and how do you write 'c-a-t.' There are thousands of things blind people have to learn, I've been told," he said, not noticing he had used the word "blind" or not letting her see he knew. He had never said it out loud before, not once.

"Anybody would hate having to—" Anna began.

"Most people," he interrupted her. "We hate to appear like fools. But I remembered the day you came and asked me why you changed the minus sign to a plus and added. You knew it was basic. All your friends got it. You knew I was studying university math so it would seem exactly like the ABCs to me. And you'd been told for years that you were a dumb cluck. Yet you had the nerve to say, 'I don't know this. Teach me.'"

Anna, also remembering back, realized that it had not really been that way at all. She had asked him because he had been crying and she had not known what else to do. So she wasn't brave, the way he thought. But she didn't contradict him.

"I really did think I couldn't help you with math when you asked me," he went on. "But this morning I saw that all mathematics happens inside somebody's head before it ends up on paper. Your mind figures it out and you write down what your mind is doing. Nothing's gone wrong with my mind!"

"No, not a thing," Anna said. "Except I thought you were going crazy."

She could say it outright now because her fear was a thing of the past. Or she hoped it was. Rudi's dark glasses hid his scarred eyes but his grin looked reassuring. He held out his hand and she took hold of it.

"I think maybe I was going a little crazy," he said, no longer smiling, but his handclasp was firm. "I was afraid. I even thought of killing myself, only I didn't know how. Then I thought of Mama . . ."

"I should hope so!" said his sister, jerking her hand free and slapping at his. "And all the rest of us too! Mind you, Suzy Hughes would probably have thought it was beautifully tragic and romantic."

"Too bad, Suzy Hughes," he said, laughing again.

Then he turned to her, putting out both hands palms up in supplication. "Teach me, Dummkopf. Teach me so when the real teachers come crowding at me, I'll have a head start on them."

"I knew you'd feel like that," Anna said, and she began. He was quicker to learn than she had been.

She phoned Mrs. Schumacher to arrange to get him another couple of talking books.

"What happened?" Mrs. Schumacher demanded.

"It was all right. But would you mind if we told Papa and Mama first? Then I'll come and tell you everything," Anna said, feeling mean but not wanting to talk anymore behind Rudi's back.

"Just knowing it's all right is enough for now," the teacher said, relief and delight mingled in her voice. "I was pretty worried. I'll get you the records. You can pick them up at our place."

Anna smuggled in the big flat boxes when nobody but Rudi was home. For the present, he listened to them only when he knew the house was empty. He had already made it clear that when he was in his room he wanted no visitors. The chiming clock downstairs helped him keep track of when the dangerous hours were drawing near.

When he had learned the alphabet, Anna got, again through Mrs. Schumacher, a book of simple stories for him to read and a Braille slate and stylus and some stiff paper so that he could learn to write. Rudi was horrified when he realized that, since he had to poke the holes through the paper from the back, he had to reverse all the letters he had just mastered, to make them come out the right way around. But when he actually tried doing it, it was not as difficult as he had imagined. Anna got pretty good at it herself, writing messages for him to figure out. Since they were both doing it, their mistakes were more amusing than discouraging.

"This way, you'll be able to take notes when you're back in college," she said, oh so casually, one afternoon.

"Listen, lady, don't rush me," Rudi warned. "I'm not nearly ready to think about—"

"Here," Anna interrupted, keeping him busy, "read this."

As the days passed, Rudi grew more and more excited and also more and more restless. Having emerged from his cocoon, he wanted to fly.

"I wish I could go OUT!" he cried, after an hour's hard work. "I feel like a bird in a cage."

Anna laughed at him. "You're the funniest-looking bird I ever saw."

Yet the next afternoon she got away from school early.

"Come on!" she said, running up to his room and banging in. "I'll take you out."

"Out? No, you won't," Rudi declared, his jaw setting.

For a moment, Anna felt so frustrated that she wanted to hit him. Then she realized he was afraid.

"I don't have time for you to get into a mood right now," she half yelled at him, keeping her flash of insight to herself. "Mama and Papa are at the store. The others are all at the final playoff rugby game between us and Bloor. They won't be home for hours. We're perfectly safe. Nobody'll know but us. Rudi, outside it's gorgeous! Crisp and smelling of bonfires . . ."

"I don't want people to see me," he said, his voice low.

"Coward!" Anna taunted. "What do you think is so special about the way you look? I'll wear dark glasses too, if it'll make you feel better. It's so sunny that nobody would think a thing about it. I'll be your cane. We can just go around the block, if you want. Come on."

"You don't have to wear dark glasses," he said, getting up slowly, his face gradually relaxing and then actually growing eager. He grinned in her direction. "You'd better not wear dark glasses, come to think of it. They'd probably make you practically as blind as I am. You have to lead me."

"Like Little Lord Fauntleroy," she teased, pulling his hand through her elbow. "Just lean on me, Grandfather."

Rudi had no trouble navigating the stairs. He had the places he went inside the house memorized by now. She opened the front door and, seeing he was wavering even yet, she tugged him through, big as he was, and slammed it behind them.

"Let's go," she said.

He lifted his head, breathed deeply the wonderful October air, took her arm, and began to walk with her.

"Thank you, Anna," he said quietly, a moment later. "I'd forgotten how it smelled."

"You're quite welcome," she said, and they turned the corner.

A couple was coming toward them. As Rudi heard the sound of approaching footsteps, he gripped her arm so tightly he hurt her. She bore it until the people had passed them.

The instant he thought they were out of earshot, he demanded, "Did those people stare at me?"

"How would I know?" Anna asked.

He stopped in his tracks and half turned to her, as though he wanted to see her face. Then he guffawed so loudly that Anna did see a woman, out raking leaves, lift her head to look. She did not mention the lady.

"It's not all that funny," she said, trying to keep from laughing herself.

"Talk about the perfect squelch!" Rudi said.

"If you still trust me, we can cross the street here and walk in the park," Anna suggested.

"I trust you," Rudi said. "But be careful."

"I'm always careful," Anna said with dignity, and they went and walked in the park, the dry leaves rustling and crackling around their feet.

When they were safely home, Rudi said, "The minute we've sprung all this on the family, how about going walking every day? It would do you a world of good."

"I already planned on that," Anna said, sounding smug and not caring if she did. "I knew you'd like it."

That night, Anna wakened in pitch blackness to feel Rudi's hand close over her mouth, stifling her inevitable scream.

"Anna," he said in a frantic whisper, "I've forgotten everything I've learned. I've been trying and trying to read but I can only get a couple of letters. I know it starts with an R and then, a little further on, there's a W and another R, but I can't recognize a single other letter. Here. You try."

Anna felt a healthy urge to slay him, blind or not. But she sat up, still in the dark, took the Braille book and found, as he said, an R, some letters she didn't recognize, and then a W.

"If it's any comfort to you," she said, "it makes no sense to me either."

She was wide awake now, sharing his consternation. As she shifted a bit to get a better grip on the bulky book, an idea came to her.

"Here," she said, shoving it back at him. "Try it now."

He stayed right there by her side and began going laboriously from letter to letter.

"O . . . N . . . E . . . D . . . A . . . Y . . . One day!" he exclaimed, amazed. "How did you do it?"

"You had the book upside down, you big idiot," she said. "R is W backward. Who's the Dummkopf now? Go away and let me sleep."

The next evening, when Rudi came downstairs after supper, he brought three sheets of Braille paper with him, hidden in an old notebook. Once the news was over, before anyone had a chance to drift away, he announced to all of them that he wished they would stay for a few minutes.

"It won't take long," he said, his voice strained. "I have something to read to you."

They sat frozen in their places, staring at him. Papa turned and looked at Anna. She, glancing around to make sure everyone was paying proper attention, caught his eye. He patted the place beside him. She got up and moved over and sat there, with his arm around her.

"We're just getting settled," she explained to her student, who after all had no way of knowing what was happening. "Now they're ready. Go ahead, Rudi."

He had been waiting for her signal, as they had arranged. He took the sheets of Braille out where the whole family could see them.

"What we picked is special," he said. "You might guess it's by Emily Dickinson, since she's Miss Sutcliff's favorite poet."

He paused, and he and Anna laughed. The others did not know how to react. They sat in bewildered silence. Rudi struggled on.

"The poem matters to me because it was through books, one talking book, that Anna first broke through my shell. We'll explain later. Anyway, these words seem to be written about me."

Resting his fingers lightly on the top line of the transcribed Braille, he began, slowly, to read.

> *"He ate and drank the precious words,*
> *His spirit grew robust;*
> *He knew no more that he was poor,*
> *Nor that his frame was dust.*
>
> *"He danced along the dingy days,*
> *And this bequest of wings*
> *Was but a book. What liberty*
> *A loosened spirit brings!"*

Even though Rudi, through repetition, knew the words, he disciplined himself to feel each letter and really read so that they could all see. Papa's arm tightened around Anna. She could feel him shaking. She twisted about and put her arms around his neck and murmured into his ear, "Isn't it wonderful to see him, Papa?"

Still holding her, he nodded, his eyes never leaving his son.

Rudi finished. There was one hushed second. Then pandemonium broke loose. All the questions, the muddled explanations, the congratulations, poured forth together. Finally Rudi stood up, put his arm around his mother's shoulders, and said to his father, although he was not quite facing him, "You can call that man from the C.N.I.B. for me tomorrow, Papa, if you don't mind."

Papa took one quiet step so that his voice would come back from where Rudi had thought he was. Anna, the only one to notice, wanted to hug him again, but stayed where she was.

257

"I'll look up the number for you but you can call him yourself, I think," Ernst Solden said.

"Yes," Rudi said, after a moment. He made his voice sound as casual as his father's had seemed to be, although neither of them fooled the other. "Yes, I think I'll do that in the morning."

24

ON THE FIRST OF NOVEMBER, when there was an almost warm day, Anna, at last, invited her three friends to drop in. Rudi boasted that he now felt strong enough to take even Suzy's adulation. They moved out onto the back porch, which looked out over their tiny yard. Rudi sat by the railing where he could feel the wind blowing. Mama, home early for the occasion, brought out a tray of cookies and coffee. Somewhere she had found nuts and currants to put into the cookies and lots of butter; she must have been saving them for a special day. The girls chattered, self-conscious at first and then more and more themselves.

Maggie told of their latest letter from her father. It had been censored in places but he was somewhere where he was freezing to death.

"He told Mother he'd give anything to cuddle up with her at night," Maggie said.

"He's probably on one of those convoys that go up through the North Sea," Rudi said. "I think I might have landed there. I wish I were with them sometimes."

The visitors were silenced by this. Mama, who was growing accustomed to the new Rudi, made a half-disapproving noise with her tongue. What she meant by it was not clear but Rudi smiled in her direction.

He reached carefully for his coffee cup.

"A little to the left," Anna said quietly.

He picked it up with ease and sipped, not acknowledging her words. This was part of life for them now. She, because of and in spite of her poor vision, seemed to have a sixth sense when it came to his needs.

She drank her own coffee, feeling pleased with the afternoon. Clouds kept coming up but they would soon pass, she hoped. Meanwhile, Mr. McNair had been over to talk to Rudi a couple of times. In the last few days, he had begun to talk about returning to college when he had really mastered Braille and had learned to move about more independently. Someone had spoken of a possible guide dog. Anna did not know how any of it would turn out but it was hopeful talk. And now both she and Rudi were sleeping at nights. He joined them for supper now and when, as was inevitable, he had knocked over his water glass one night, he had been the first to say, with a laugh, what Mama had said for years.

"It's only water and an extra washing won't hurt anyone in this family."

Suddenly Rudi lifted his face to the sky.

"The sun's come out again," he said.

Mama looked startled. Suzy blurted, "How do *you* know?"

"Oh, I have my secret methods," Rudi said, his voice light and teasing.

Anna looked at the warm sunlight touching his cheeks and wondered how sighted people could be so stupid.

"It's really clearing up," she said, ignoring Suzy. "The sky is turning a lovely bright blue in the east."

"And the birds?" Rudi said, turning his head to where she sat. "Are you listening for their singing still, Anna?"

"Oh, they came out of their shells long ago," she told him, choosing her words with care. "They're grown now and starting their journey toward the sun."

Rudi did not answer at once, and in that stretched silence Anna knew, deep inside herself, how hard everything still was for her brother, how unsure and alone and afraid he often felt.

"It's a long way," he said at last.

She heard the slight drag in his voice, but she also saw he was smiling at her just a little, letting her know he understood.

"I think they'll make it," said Anna.

"Maybe," Rudi said. Then he took a deep breath and added, "You know . . . they just might."